*   *   *

I've tried to just back away from Marvin but something just draws me even closer. I'm intrigued by his inhibition and adventurous nature. It's like an addiction. I try to stay away from him but the more I try, the harder it gets to resist.

Once, he showed up at my son's birthday party and we ended up fucking in the bathroom. I couldn't help it. He cornered me. Just like now, he's in the den watching the football game with my husband, and I'm trying to figure out how I can suck his dick without raising suspicions.

I hate that Jason (my husband) befriended him when we bought this fucking house. Every time I walk into my private sitting room, I think of how he made me orgasm. Jason thinks I go in there for solitude, for a place away from him and the kids. I go in that room to cum over and over again at the thought of Marvin. Jason has no idea I spend my time making videos for Marvin to view. Nor does he know…

*   *   *

STICKY SECRETS 2

An Urban Anthology of Erotic Romance

Purple Spider Legs

By E. Scrill

Holy Fucking Secrets

By Fauzykiss

Who's The Boss?

By Kaylynn Hunt

Only For One Night

By Sylvia Hubbard

STREET INK PUBLICATIONS®

 TM

This is a work of fiction. Names, characters, places, and incidents either are the product of the author's imagination or are used fictitiously, and any resemblance to actual person, living or dead, business establishments, events, or locales, is entirely coincidental.

If you are purchasing this book, you are 18 or older. Thank you.

ISBN: 978-0-9816399-2-5

First Edition

Manufactured in the United States of America.

**Follow our sponsors on instagram
@thehoneycoco**

**I would like to give a shout out to
our graphic artist, Clif Wilson.
Follow on instagram
@3rd_sun_entertainment.**

**Our gorgeous cover model,
Gabrielle Caple, appears courtesy of
Rude & Rich Clothing. Follow her
on**

IG @Via_beautyy

SC @ Via_beautii

STICKY SECRETS 2:

An Urban Anthology of Erotic Romance

Purple Spider Legs

Chapter 1

Tracy Parks eased his Caddy into a spot at the pharmacy across from Teresa's Place. Usually, he parked on Six mile, but lately he had been the target of a disgruntled stalker he'd met on Instagram. After having her in every which way, Tracy decided that the overweight woman no longer peaked his interest and blocked her calls. He doubted that he would be able to enjoy having a drink unless his ride was under the protective dome light of the security guard who was strategically placed in the alley across the street to watch over the cars of bar patrons who parked at the curb and pharmacy lot.

Once inside the bar, Tracy spotted his homie, Fat Mike, down at the end of the bar. Fat Mike was leaning close to Juli, an attractive young woman with an angelic face. As Fat Mike spoke into her ear, Juli smiled while slowly shaking her head. Tracy smiled, knowing his homie was more than likely telling her something tripped out. Fat Mike was known to get the party crackin', and could talk a cat off a fish cart.

Tracy zig-zagged through the moderate crowd until he reached his homie. "What's goin' on, bro?"

"Been trying to get Juli to come chill and have a drink with me at the crib, but she actin' all boojy! I'm about ready to just give up and leave her sad."

Juli playfully rolled her eyes and said, "Well, gone then. You used to talk to my girl so you know I am not about to go to your apartment to drink or nothin' else…"

Fat Mike looked at her with a cunning grin. "See, that was a long time ago, and y'all probly don't even talk no more. You know you had a crush on me since before you had hair on it!"

8

Juli almost choked as she sipped her wine.

"...I stay fresh, plus I'm the best lookin' nigga in the bar!" Fat Mike sported a victorious grin, leaving Juli in a fit of laughter as he led Tracy to an empty table.

Tracy watched as Mike flipped through a dozen pictures in his cell phone.

Mike's eyes widened with excitement. "Here it is! Look at that!"

Tracy leaned toward the phone's screen. "What? It's just a chick twerkin'."

"Man, look at that ass! She lookin' way better than that pigeon-toed chick you was cakin' with last week!"

"Aww, man, beat it! I thought you had somethin' to show me."

Mike lowered his phone and jerked his head around when he heard the voice of their good friend, Bull. Bull lived in their 'hood, but only came around sometimes. He had a heavy New York accent and when the conversation started to get dull, Bull would spice things up with his tales of growing up in Brooklyn.

"What y'all fags in here doin'?" Bull asked as he walked toward the two with a huge grin.

Mike folded his arms and stood in a D-boy stance. "What up, my dog? In here showin' Tee some pics from the other night."

Tracy sucked his teeth then said, "Man, them shots look like you was at some biker afterhour!"

With a smile, Bull said, "Let's see!"

Mike didn't hesitate to show his pictures.

Bull's eyes widened. "Oh, that's ol' girl!"

Mike turned towards Tracy with a told-ya-so grin.

Tracy was still unconvinced of what Mike was saying, so he asked Bull, "Ol' girl, who?"

"Yeah! She outside about to come in. She was parking when I came in."

Mike flashed every tooth in his head. "I'm about to get her! She was on my nuts last time I saw her!"

Tracy looked around to see what caused Mike's smile to quickly vanish. He watched Mike turn to a young woman coming closer, wearing a tee shirt with jeans that had stylish rips. Mike began to blush as the woman neared. Tracy held his smile a bit better than Bull as the young woman kept past Mike.

With the nonchalant attitude obviously not working, Mike switched gears and reached for the woman's arm. "Hey, you remember me?"

The woman seemed startled by Mike's touch. "Oh, I didn't even see you right there. I remember you."

Mike released her arm. "I thought you was comin' in here lookin' for me or somethin'." He cheesed, awaiting her response.

"Naw, we talked about that the last time I ran into you."

Mike looked baffled. "What we say? I don't remember."

"You don't remember me tellin' you that I already got a dude?"

"Well, what you doin' in here? This spot is for females that like to get smacked on the ass!" Mike sported a cheap smile as if he was wondering how she would respond to his comment.

She twisted her lips then said, "I don't know about that. I'm just here to meet my girl, Juli."

Mike watched as the curvaceous woman stepped away. "Oh, you with her?"

Juli peeked her head around her friend who was now taking a seat next to her. "Yes, she is!"

Tracy leaned close to Mike and Bull. "Well, I guess you can forget about both of them."

Mike interrupted Bull and Tracy's taunting chuckles when he asked Bull, "So, what's up? You need some weed?"

"What's the name of it today; purple spider legs?"

"The name don't even matter. You know if Fats got it, it's the bomb!"

"Yeah, whatever! Here, gimme a forty."

Mike looked to Tracy. "You see the shit I gotta go through 'cause I'm his friend?" Mike turned back to Bull. "I sell fifties and hundreds!"

"Man, I don't wanna hear that. Fix me up!" Bull laughed with Tracy as they watched Mike march toward the rear exit to retrieve his goods. Bull turned to Tracy. "It's two right there for us.

What you wanna do? Don't tell me you scared."
Without giving Tracy time to respond, Bull
continued with, "Awww, shit! Wait 'til I tell
Mike."

        "Get outta here! Ol' girl said she got a
man."

        "Aww, that don't mean nothin'! Like Mike
said, 'this where they come when they want a
smack on the ass'."

        "Okay, well, when you gonna get on Juli?"

        Bull turned and started toward the women.
"Can I buy y'all a drink?"

        "You can buy me one. She's about to leave.
Tracy, can you walk my girl to the car?"

        Tracy's antennas went up. He hadn't paid
her too much attention before with Fat Mike
attempting to claim her and all, but now, he could
tell what all the fuss was about. The woman wasn't
very pretty, but not at all ugly. She could best be
described as sexy with a divalicious flair.

        Her body was a completely different story.
She was short and petite, but bottom-heavy. Her
exploding hips complimented her perfectly plump
rear deliciously. Tracy knew that inside of those

ripped jeans was explicit content and he wanted some of it. A lot of it.

Tracy followed closely as the woman led him out the front door of the bar. He couldn't help but see the sensual swaying of the woman's back pockets. He knew someone had to be having a ball making it with the young sexpot.

"I'm across the street," the woman began. "If you don't mind, could you see me over there? I do not trust those guys over there smoking weed."

Tracy didn't mind a few more minutes with her so he told her, "Oh, yeah. I got you. I used to do this all the time when I was a crossing guard back in fifth grade."

She gave a smile and a playful elbow to Tracy's side which made him feel like he had a better chance than Fat Mike. He definitely knew he had a much better chance than the guys smoking weed in the parking lot.

A dull flash in Tracy's peripheral vision caught his eye. It was the sun's glimmer on one of the woman's shoes. It looked like they were made of some sort of reflective fabric.

"What are you looking at?" the woman asked Tracy.

"Just checking out your shoes. They look like some shiny gym shoes."

"Yeah, they're okay."

"They look expensive."

"Yeah, I guess so. They were a gift."

"Tracy noticed that the woman didn't seem to be in a rush to get in her vehicle, so he continued with, "Well, I know you got somebody that like you a lot—gettin' gifts and thangs."

"Yup, but too bad he had to go away for a little while."

Yes! Tracy thought, knowing that she meant that he was enlisted or in the joint, and either way it seemed like he had a chance with her. "Damn, that's too bad. So, why you leavin'?"

"I gotta get my kids from the sitter's."

"How many you got?"

"Two."

He held out his hand. "By the way, my name is Tracy."

"I'm Kim."

15

"Well, Kim, you think you might wanna go to a concert or something some time?"

"Are you trying to take me on a date?"

"I know you got a man, but I figure you might wanna have fun sometimes while he's gone."

"We still together, but I have been lookin' for a friend and you seem like a nice guy."

"That works for me. Let's just be friends."

The two exchanged numbers, then Tracy went back across the street towards the bar. He was met at the door by Fat Mike.

Mike raised his eyebrows. "Did she give you the number?"

"Yup," Tracy triumphantly announced.

"You ain't gon' get that!" Mike said as he moved to the side to let Tracy pass.

Like always, Mike came up with a group of newly met females who drank and smoked weed, but had neither. The sun had set, and Tracy and Bull wasted no time in getting to know the women before Mike did something to piss them off.

Tracy's cellphone jangled in his pocket. "Hello?"

"Hey, this Kim."

It was two shots of vodka and a blunt after meeting the young woman that Tracy figured he'd never hear from so it took a few seconds to remember. "Oh, what's up? I ain't think I was gon' hear from you."

"Why is that? We did say we were going to be friends. I was just calling to let you know that I'm ready for you."

Ready for me? Hmmm! "Okay, cool. So what you got up?"

"Nothin' really. I don't have a baby-sitter and I just put my kids to sleep. Juli already let me know that you were a nice guy and safe to have over. You can come by and smoke with me if you want."

Hell yeah! Good 'ol Juli! I'm gonna have to add that girl to my Christmas list! "Okay, well I can be on the way in a minute. Text me your address." Tracy slid the cellphone back into his pocket and started toward Fat Mike to grab a bag of purple spider legs. He had lost all interest in the new group of chicks Mike now had, remembering how sexy Juli's friend was.

17

Chapter 2

In his 2015 Dodge pickup, Tracy cruised toward the address Kim gave. He casually sipped vodka and cranberry from a plastic cup and thought of how sexy she was with her fair skin and petite body. She may have been a small woman, but had enough curves where it counted.

As he parked in front of the house, he received a text telling him to pull into the driveway. He gladly did, feeling like his ride would be a lot safer. He had no idea if Kim's neighborhood was lousy with car thieves.

Tracy could smell the wonderful aroma of barbecue as he walked up the driveway into the backyard. When he reached the back, he found

Kim standing at a smoking grill with a tee shirt and the most appetizing short-shorts.

Kim flashed a winning smile. "Hi. You hungry? I got some steaks on."

With his eyes still glued to Kim's hips and rear, Tracy replied, "Uh, yeah. That sounds good!"

"What's wrong? What are you staring at?" Kim asked with a smirk.

"I think you know! Girl, you sexy as hell!" Tracy admitted.

"Is that right? Well, you gonna give me a hug?" she asked.

Tracy neared and couldn't help but remember Kim telling him that she was ready for him. He wasn't sure exactly what she meant, but hoped since he was over so soon after meeting her that sex was in the forecast. He knew the best way to tell if he had a green light.

Wrapping his arms around her body, he began cupping and squeezing her unguarded softness with his hands. Her welcoming hug was a green light for sure. Tracy felt his manhood begin to swell and poke out. He didn't give a damn. He wanted her to know what she was doing to him.

She felt so good that he wished he knew her well enough to kiss her.

He went ahead and released her, realizing that she was in no rush to let go, and that the steaks were still on the fire.

The two sat on the steps of the back porch with the grill in view and got to know one another as they puffed purple spider legs twisted in rolling papers. Tracy was happy to find that Kim's guy would be gone for at least the next three years due to an agreement with the courts in response to President Trump's efforts to beef up his military. So, instead of jail time, the guy was able to serve in the military for his non-violent offenses.

Tracy was certain that the guy was very happy with the deal since it meant he would receive pay and could take up a trade with no bars confining him, but was still losing because his repetition of letters was obviously failing at keeping his old lady satisfied.

Kim was horny and Tracy was certain when she told him, "I'm a freak, and I ain't had none in a year. It's a shame I'm telling you this, but I just need somebody to talk to sometimes. Sommer's daddy been gone since I was pregnant with her and I just never messed with anybody else."

Tracy didn't want to say anything. He just wanted to hear more of what she was saying. But to keep from seeming uninterested, he told her, "It's cool. I know just what you're talkin' 'bout. I'm a freak, too."

"Yeah, I been being the good girl and that shit just ain't what I'm feelin' right now. I love that nigga, but damn, he got hisself caught-up. I'm taking good care of his daughter, and I'm taking care of him, but..." She slowly shook her head.

"But that pussy gettin' hot!" Tracy interjected, feeling like he'd been around Fat Mike too long. She blushed with guilt and that let Tracy know he was right, so he reached over and slid his hand up past Kim's thighs and pressed it against her heated core as he mashed his lips against hers. He knew he may not be the best judge of character, and that he'd just met her, but if he was going to catch something from a kiss, he wanted the woman giving it to him to look like Kim.

Tracy's tongue entered Kim's mouth and assaulted hers with amorous haste.

"I gotta get the steaks," Kim said as she grabbed the rail and pulled herself up off the step.

Tracy's eyes were glued to Kim's hips and ass. He sipped his vodka to suppress the want to

21

bend her over the porch steps and make like a porn star. He wanted to put something on his stomach before trying anything slick to make sure he kept his liquor intake in check.

Purple spider legs chased the grilled steak meal as Tracy and Kim got to know one another even better. The two sat on the floor of Kim's den, in front of the television. They rested with their backs against a couch and Tracy's arm held Kim close. The television might as well have been off because he had no idea what was on. She felt so good next to him.

Her lips were the sexiest and Tracy used his to seize hers and commence a sugary dance. Kim leaned toward Tracy and eased him back onto the floor as she maneuvered on top of him. Their faces were still connected at the lips.

Tracy pushed his hand down the back of Kim's shorts into her panties and began caressing and squeezing her buns. He could feel his penile head grow and peek out past the elastic on his boxer briefs.

While in Tracy's grasp, Kim began to grind against his hardened bulge. Tracy remembered Kim undoing the top button on her shorts after their dinner, so he went ahead and began sliding them

down. He rolled her over on her back as he pulled
the shorts off over her feet.

Tracy opened Kim's legs as he mounted her,
glimpsing her pouting vulva. Coarse stubble
surrounded the brilliantly painted earth tones of
Kim's treasure. He leaned forward and gripped her
bottom lip with both of his.

Tracy found her drooling entrance and
probed her slowly. He had been told by a few other
women that he was their first in months, but once he
began entering Kim, he knew they all lied. Her
snugness couldn't be duplicated by a woman
clenching her vaginal muscles. She had that good-
good!

Tracy treaded carefully, knowing that a
mere hiccup could cause him to prematurely spend,
and he was nowhere near ready. Kim was not
helping him hold on at all. Her fingers digging into
his back from the joyous pain gave him even greater
pleasure. She moaned and pumped back beneath
him. He could feel her stubble pricking him at the
base of his shaft every time he thrust back into her,
which made him remember the beautifully drawn
honeypot that was making his day.

Kim must've been able to feel the
ejaculating jerks of Tracy's pipe and pulled his face

close as she stuck her tongue into his mouth and kissed him passionately.

Chapter 3

The day after Tracy's experience with Kim, he went to his daily hustle, serving packs of heroin. He got word from his aunt that her boyfriend had overdosed, and while cleaning out his things, she discovered a half-kilo of Mexican mud. Tracy assured her that she would be well-compensated after he moved it. It was sticky and gooey so he kept it in the freezer until he was ready to mix it with the stuff he got from his regular connect.

His cellphone started ringing in the early morning and he knew the dope fiends were ready to start their day. He had people in and out until noon. As things began to slow up for a minute, he thought about the splendid time he had the day before.

He checked his clean phone to see if Kim had bothered to call or text. He knew she was at work, but he hoped he was just as heavy on her mind as she was on his.

Nothing.

He sat that phone down and continued to grind. He had cameras around his spot to see what was going on around him on the outside.

Tracy began mixing another batch of dope since his blow-filled baggy was getting low. He mixed and cut his heroin, then wrapped each twenty-dollar blow in a piece of a lottery ticket. He filled his plastic sack with the work, then sat back and watched his security camera monitor. He had it posted right next to his television, but the television wasn't on. He sometimes just sat and scoped out the monitor until someone else came to cop.

Tracy perked when he heard his other phone vibrate on the table across the room. He felt himself smiling. He pranced over to the phone. Disappoint washed over him when he saw Fat Mike's number on the caller I.D. "What up, doe," he asked Mike.

"You comin' to the bar? Got some girls comin'!" Mike said in an animated way.

"What time you talkin' about?" Tracy asked, knowing well that Mike wanted him to be a wingman as usual--to be used in one of Mike's well-rehearsed skits that were orchestrated to separate the women after filling their skulls with caviar hopes.

"When you get here. I ain't goin' nowhere. I'm grindin' anyway."

Tracy knew that he and Mike were cool, but Mike would call Bull when the better-looking chicks came through because Bull would make sure that everyone had the pricey Patron Margarita's in their hands; making Mike look more like the key to answered prayers. Tracy realized that when he was called, the chicks consistently scored seven's at the most. But, he never hesitated to come, because due to Mike's mental priming he had received enough toe-curling oral from the nickels that he always arrived prepared to keep them knee-deep in at least vodka and cranberries.

Tracy stayed at his money spot until the sun went down, then made a bundle of blows for his Uncle Mike. His uncle used, but would still make sure his business was taken care of. Tracy headed for the bar to meet Fat Mike and his prospects.

Tracy received a text message so he checked his phone. He was so eager to read it that he pulled over. Kim's gorgeous face filled the cellphones screen, and her selfie worked far better than words could have. Tracy couldn't stop smiling. He stepped on the gas.

Once in the bar, Tracy spotted Fat Mike in a booth near the back. He was sitting with two females who looked to be under the influence of purple spider legs. Tracy wasted time with them as he sipped vodka and cranberry. The women were from Atlanta and were just trying to have fun.

For the next few days, Tracy and Fat Mike hung out with the two women and showed them around the Detroit. Tracy had only received greetings from Kim with no real convo. He still wanted some more of her.

Tracy was at his uncle's house when Kim texted him a message to come over if he wasn't busy.

"Unc, I'm gonna leave you with three bundles this time just in case I can't make it back if you need me," Tracy said, preparing himself for whatever Kim might have planned for the two of them. He had never left his uncle with as much dope at once, but knew that he had no plans of rushing away from Kim.

"Okay, young fella. I'm gonna hold it down."

Tracy didn't think his uncle sounded very convincing, but his want for Kim had his male parts beginning to solidify. With his jogging pants on, catching a boner in front of his uncle would have been disastrous, so he double-timed it toward the door, snatched open the screen, then headed out.

Tracy wrapped his arms around his friend. She was the perfect fit. She squeezed him back for a minute before they released one another. He looked into her eyes as she rubbed the dick-print in his pants. She was just as ready to do it as he was. He gripped one of her butt cheeks with one hand and started the other hand between her legs. She stood wide-legged, allowing his fingers roaming room.

Tracy kissed and fondled Kim until she gasped and pulled away. She gripped his hand and led him to a set of stairs. "Ssshh!" she began in a whisper. "My kids are sleep."

The stairs creaked as Tracy followed up into the darkness. Once inside Kim's bedroom, the kissing and fondling began again. Tracy watched as Kim's shadowy figure undressed by moonlight. He followed suit.

Kim seized Tracy's hand and led him to the bed. They stood for a minute as Tracy slid his hands all over Kim's naked body.

This bitch's body is perfect! he thought. Tracy's manhood pointed upward and pulsed with throbbing want.

Kim playfully pulled Tracy's erection down and released it, allowing it to spring up and slap his stomach. She then crawled onto the bed and rested on her knees and elbows.

No one had to tell Tracy to follow. He was on his way behind her before she was settled in place. He rested on his knees, rubbing Kim's perfect rear.

He found her slippery entrance, then slowly slipped into her. By the third stroke, Tracy's whole pubic area was wet. That was about the time that he realized he was going to need a dose of her at least every other day. He gripped her by the waist with one hand and put the other on her hip. He pulled her back into him over and over again, picking up the pace until Kim began moaning deeply. Tracy reached forward and pulled Kim's arms from under her, prompting her to rest on her face. He then grasped her hips with both hands and worked her out violently as she moaned and winced until he reached ecstasy.

Tracy showered with Kim, then helped her change the damp sheets. They cuddled in the bed, listening to The Dramatics and groups from that era as Kim's soft hand caressed and roamed any part of Tracy it could reach.

As Kim begin to snore, he slowly eased out of bed and dressed. He clumsily made his exit, tripping over children's shoes and action figures until he reached the door.

The pace picked up slightly with Kim, going from one rendezvous a week to two. Three weeks after being allowed into Kim's bed, Tracy found himself growing fond of her. Her home had no type of air conditioning, only a basic box fan, but that seemed to serve well immediately after doing the sex, when Tracy was erupting sweat. He would lie on the carpet in front of the fan and cool off while Kim started the shower.

He needed more of her but had no idea how to go about getting it. He knew she was feeling him, but that still wasn't helping him in his need to be on top of her a few more times a week.

With heroin reaching epidemic levels in and around Detroit, Tracy started eating a little better than before. He was a slave to the trade. His clientele needed their stuff when they needed it, and he knew he had better keep them fixed or else he could lose them. And for each one lost, he would be that much closer to his poverty-stricken roots.

With the growth of Tracy's pockets, Kim's appetite leaned farther to the finer side. He quickly learned he could lure her with dinner dates. And she definitely ate her fill. Her hips and ass was where she stored most of the extra growth. Tracy loved every inch of her increased thickness. She felt a little better when he lay on top and sank into her. She could take it with her legs a little higher in the air. And if on her knees, she could withstand the pounding with her rear arched higher.

Tracy and Kim would meet over the next couple of months at different eateries around where she worked. And more often than not, she received the bat and balls while on her lunch breaks.

Christmas was near and Tracy was ready to surprise Kim with a pocket full of mistletoe or anything that could get him more of her kisses and affection. One day, he found himself overcome with thoughts of the things he had done to her the night before. He normally didn't hit her two days in a row, but on that particular occasion, he had shook from his lust-filled haze only after he was standing in the showroom of the dealership where she worked downtown with a fistful of daisies.

Kim walked out into the showroom after being paged. Tracy stood with his back to her, trying to seem as if he were more interested in the pamphlets in the rack.

"May I help you?" Tracy heard Kim's voice say.

He turned to her and held out the flowers, not so certain anymore if he was doing the right thing with Kim's confidence-shattering demeanor.

"Oh, you gon' try to come with some flowers after you all on the internet with some bitch?"

Internet? Huh? Tracy thought. He had no clue as to what was going on. He thought he was about to get some pussy-getting points. Instead, he was somehow in the red. "Look, just take these flowers and we'll figure it all out later. I can't walk outta here past the people who was out there clapping for me with the same flowers!"

Kim snatched the flowers and smashed them across Tracy's head. In the end, he still walked out with the flowers himself, except now he was wearing them.

For the next few days, Tracy made record profits in the streets. All the while, he was cranky and irritable. He was missing Kim. He had tried to talk to her and find out what she saw on social media about him that ticked her off so much, but she would only say, "Don't play me like that! I saw the picture. But, don't worry about it, boo."

It had to be one of them dingbat broads Mike had who posted some shit! Tracy thought.

He wasn't going to sweat her. None of his texts were ever responded to, so he realized there was no point in trying to call…after the first eight times.

Tracy walked into the bar, and as he neared the booth Fat mike and Bull were sitting in, he heard Bull ask while looking at Mike's cellphone, "What is it, a booty hole?"

"Naw, fool!" Mike began. "It's a nipple!" He gave Bull a few minutes to scrutinize the picture in the cellphone. He turned to Tracy and changed the conversation. "Do you still talk to Juli's friend?"

"Sometimes," he lied, knowing that if Mike knew that his fling was over, Mike would rejoice since he wanted Kim in the first place. In an attempt to quickly move to something else, Tracy asked, "Did you see my tow truck yet?"

"Tow truck?" Mike asked. "Why would you get a tow truck and you don't even got a house? You gonna be on the front seat makin' Spam sandwiches." Mike knew Tracy was gettin' money but still had to try to get a laugh some kind of a way.

Bull sat upright. "Word? You got it outside, right now?"

"Yup. It's in the lot."

The three went outside.

Bull smiled, then said, "Damn, you got the winch to get people outta ditches and everything. You can hustle good in this! I like it."

By the time Detroit was blanketed by tormenting January snows, Tracy had bundles of heroin rolling out of his spot on Benson, manned by his uncle Mike. He also had a spot on the west side, but had his cousin, Shudricka, holding it down. With cameras all around, she could see everyone walking up to cop. Normally, a single female wouldn't be trusted to work a spot selling something as needed as heroin, but Tracy had a system in place where no one knew who was serving them because they had to insert the money in the milk chute and close the door before the door on the inside where Shudricka was could be opened.

35

She would then take the cash and leave the purchased amount of dope before closing the milk chute back, so there was no way the fiends could know whether or not they were being served by Tracy himself. But, Shudricka still had a pistol-grip pump at hands-reach. Tracy's biggest task was making sure the spots were flush with product. He usually stayed up until the wee hours of the morning making blows for his spots.

With his bag flowing, Tracy had time to hustle in his tow truck. He would cruise the city and find all kinds of people in despair. Most were women with simple issues like flat tires or empty fuel tanks. But every now and again, he would encounter a woman with a serious problem that would require a tow, and half the time they couldn't afford it. Of course, those were the times Fat Mike loved to be present.

Tracy would let Mike roll with him while he hustled, just to have company, because he knew Mike wasn't going to lift a finger to unscrew a gas cap. But, Mike would keep his antennas up for the desperate women who were stranded. Tracy knew he had to cut that out after Mike's indecent proposal.

A Chevy Impala was wrecked on the side of the Davidson freeway one night. Tracy pulled over behind the Impala and took an incoming call.

"I'm about to go see if they need help," Mike said as he exited through the passenger door.

By the time Tracy was done with his call and began toward Mike and the Impala, he could hear, "...I mean, I'm tryin' to help you, but you know what I want...and my mans, too!"

"Hey, bro, let me do this," Tracy interjected. "I'm sorry. He's used to dealing with strippers."

Tracy knew giving the woman a free tow would be the best option. He and Mike argued all the way home.

Mike being Mike, saved the best for last. As soon as Tracy pulled into his driveway to drop him off, Mike told him, "Yeah, man, thanks for fuckin' up our head for the night! Now, I gotta go in here and argue and panty-wrestle with this crazy bitch 'cause she still mad about some dumb-ass scratches I had on my arm the other day! Don't ask for my help no mo'!" Mike slammed the door and stepped toward his house.

"What help?" Tracy yelled.

Mike couldn't hear him. He was now on his porch entering his house. He had won the argument. The worst part was that Mike at least had a possible in the house, and Tracy was horny with nothing going on for the night.

He knew what he wanted. He knew where she was. He also knew he hadn't heard from her. Knowing that he was forewarned of her current relationship, he knew that there was nothing he could say, and that he should just bury his feelings. He couldn't help but think, *I bet she got a new friend!*

Tracy didn't want to go out like a stalker, but he really wanted to drive by Kim's place--just to see what he could see. He knew he would never hear the last of it if Fat Mike and Bull found out he was just a side-nigga doing drive-bys.

Fuck that, I'm in a tow truck, he remembered as he headed in the direction of Kim's house, prepared to fabricate the details if he were to get caught on his mission. *She is not gonna know whether or not somebody around the block needed a tow,* he grinned.

With his alibi in place, Tracy slowly crept up Kim's block, only to find her son's father's truck in the driveway.

That bitch! He was glad he'd peeked through the blinds on the occasion when he was over and the guy came to pick up his son, so Tracy knew his vehicle. He was certain Kim was being pounded-out since the baby daddy was over after two a.m. with no lights on.

Tracy headed home, disappointed, but glad he had found out the real.

Damn, her other baby daddy don't even know she cheatin' on us!

Chapter 4

By the time spring had colored the city green, Tracy had found his way into the veins of white America. His money was made from his spots, so aside from chillin' with the fellas, he cruised in his tow truck. Most of the time, he found himself in some kind of grimy, overall outfit. His fingernails constantly accumulated some type of soot-like substance underneath them. Every now and then, he got a chance to get fresh.

Along with the good weather, summertime meant concerts at the Aretha Franklin Amphitheater, an open-air venue situated on the Detroit River under a large tarp. The stage was positioned close enough to the water for boaters to pull up and enjoy the show.

Tracy gave a tow to a customer one day, and for outstanding service, the guy told Tracy that he was a concert promoter and blessed him with two tickets to an old-school concert on the river. He had plenty to wear, but no date.

The day of the show, Tracy was decked out in fresh linen with the tightest fade. He even went ahead and pulled out his jewels. He was ready, but still didn't have a date.

He decided to swing by the bar to see if anyone else wanted to use the ticket so it wouldn't go to waste. As soon as he walked in, there was Fat Mike, up to his old tricks.

Mike was in a woman's ear saying, "Well, if it's too late after we leave my house, we can still go to the casino to get some chili dogs." Mike turned to Tracy, then said, "Yeah, man, I ain't forget about the concert. My new woman right here ain't gonna let me go."

The woman's face spun around to face Mike.

"Man, you frontin'!" Tracy said.

"Naw, naw. I got her cousin in there ready to go with you!"

The woman put her hand on her hip. "So, you gon' just pimp my cuz out now?"

"Just be glad I'm keepin' that for myself!" Fat Mike said as he administered a slap to the woman's rear. "...Cuz I'll pimp yo' ass out, too!" He turned and led Tracy to a booth which was occupied by the Greek Goddess, Aphrodite. "Let's go blow one," Mike told her. She got up and followed the three outside to the parking lot.

Mike waved everyone to the side of the booth in the lot. The attendant, Rapp, sat in the booth. (He was called Rapp because that's what he called everyone else, and he really didn't do anything interesting that day, or that month, for that matter. He's just included in the story so that he doesn't talk junk when I go back to the bar.) Mike lit a blunt filled with purple spider legs and took a few tokes, then passed it to Aphrodite's cousin.

"Girl, do you know this nigga done arranged a date with you and that man?" said the cousin to Aphrodite before taking a drag on the blunt.

The goddess creased her angelic face when she questioned, "A date?" She looked to Tracy, then back to Mike.

"Yeah," Mike began. "Don't you like old school concerts?"

Tracy received the blunt and took a puff. He looked at Aphrodite's enticing lips. In his peripheral vision, he could see his diamond wristband inhaling the sun and exhaling blue and red sparks. He took a real slow hit as an excuse to keep his arm raised.

Aphrodite looked to Tracy and asked, "What was your name again?" making the disastrous mistake of keeping her eyes locked to the fireworks on Tracy's wrist too long.

I'm putting my dick in her mouth, he thought, realizing that he had a goddess in his snare. "Tracy."

The concert was the perfect first date. The weather was perfect, and so was Tracy's date. She held his arm possessively as they eased through the crowded theatre toward their seats. To make things better, Tracy could see Pejoe coming his way.

Pejoe was cool with all the fellas in the 'hood and would come through and trip out if he wasn't busy doing his thang in the streets. He was always in competition with Tracy some kind of way. He might win on the pool table but would be victimized on the chess board. Just like Tracy, Pejoe had plenty money and street power. He was getting closer, and he had Kim on his arm.

The two slapped five and kept it moving.

Tracy now knew why he hadn't heard from Kim. She was wasting her good lovin' on Pejoe. *Fuck her!* he thought, remembering the goddess on his arm. He was really looking forward to getting to know her.

The following winter was wretched, laced with aggravating snows and Arctic winds. Power outages were common, and to make matters worse, dope fiends were out robbing the workers who were trying to repair the downed electric lines.

Winter weather advisories were constant on the radio and T.V. that day and Tracy was out reaping the benefits of having a tow truck. After being irritated with the petty and penniless in the 'hood, Tracy decided to take his grind up I-75. He knew he was bound to make money in Oakland County, which was one of the wealthiest in America.

Receiving countless praises, Tracy used his winch to yank dollar bills from icy ditches. Tracy ignored his hunger pangs and proceeded to drop off his last customer for the night. While passing Crooks road, he was being waved down by a figure on the side of the freeway. Tracy slowed as his passenger slowly rolled down the window.

"Help me, please!" Tracy heard a familiar voice say. The figure's face got close to the window. "I slid off the road and my car is stuck over there! I can't get any cellphone service either."

It was Kim!

"Tracy, man, I'm so glad to see you…"

"Yeah, we can chop it up later," he began. "I'm with a customer right now."

"Please, come back when you get done with her," she speed-talked.

Tracy stomped the gas pedal and sped away while watching Kim trudge through the snow back toward her car which was fixed in a snow bank. He was thrilled at the thought of Kim being at his mercy and tried not to scare his passenger as he made haste through the snow, nearly fish-tailing and what not, taking the vehicle to the destination.

Tracy's manhood swelled as he neared Kim, sitting helpless in her car. He had made more than his quota doing tows, so the cash wasn't an issue. He was ready to have some real fun.

"What seems to be the problem, ma'am?" Tracy joked as he neared Kim's open driver door.

"Boy, you don't know how happy I am to see you!" Kim said, forcing a fraudulent laugh.

"Yeah, I been out here grindin' all day and now it's time to take it in. You see I'm about the last tow truck out here."

"I know, I been out here for over an hour with no phone service!"

"I hope you got some money, 'cause I really don't wanna help you since you can't never call a nigga," Tracy said, changing the feel of the conversation.

"Huh? C'mon now, don't even start that! How much is it gonna cost to get me outta here?"

Tracy rubbed his chin. "Hmmm. Let me think…"

"Look, I'm just trying to get back on the road. I got one hundred and seventy-three dollars."

Tracy creased his face as if he were in pain. "Ouch! So close! See, the cheapest I can go on that is one hundred seventy-six!"

"What? C'mon! It's only about twenty or thirty feet to the road!"

"So! And, this is only a dick," Tracy said while cupping his crotch. "What you wanna do?"

"Tracy, please! I'm seeing somebody. I can't do that."

"Well, fuck it! Call Pejoe to get yo' ass out then!" Tracy turned and started toward his truck.

Kim sprang up from the driver's seat and started for the road in an attempt to flag down a passing vehicle. She slipped and nearly slid under Tracy's tow truck. Kim looked in both directions and saw no sign of another car. "You fuckin' bitch!" she sobbed as she dusted the snow off of her pants.

Tracy stood at Kim's open driver door after she got in, waiting patiently to see how she would play things out. He watched as she slid her hands in her pants at the hips, raising up slightly to allow them to slide down.

"Hold up," Tracy began while unzipping his fly. "You know I'm getting old and my dick don't work right all the time. You gonna have to help me out!" he announced, smiling with his words.

"Man, c'mon, Tracy!"

Tracy reached in his undies and released his antagonist.

"It, it look pretty hard to me," she stammered with a nervous look on her face. "Okaaay!" she whined as he grabbed a handful of her expertly coiffed hair and pulled her face to his crotch.

Tracy never experienced oral from Kim and didn't know what to expect. That didn't stop him from pushing himself between her lips and into her mouth. With his dick warm, he didn't care if the rest of his body turned blue from the cold.

With her mouth full, Kim went to work on Tracy, proving that she was a superior fellatrix. Her hums and controlled slurps were getting the best of him. Just as he began to wonder…

Oh my GOD! She swallowed it! Tracy sheathed his private parts and turned for his truck. "I'm about to hook you up so I can get you outta here."

Tracy gave Kim the help she needed without a word. He didn't give a damn about her anymore. He had a goddess waiting for him, and he also had one up on Pejoe in case he ever decided to talk junk!

THE END

After doing time in a Michigan prison for guns and 20 pounds of green stuff, author E. Scrill received a 2006 parole. He scraped together enough for a hundred-book print run and began selling his debut novel, Drug Lords, in the cash-strapped streets of Detroit. He traded his inked magic for money, and in 2007 founded Street Ink Publications. We are currently reviewing works by other up and coming authors.

Follow E. Scrill on Facebook: @book man

Instagram @author_e_scrill_

Other books by E. Scrill :

Drug Lords

Children of the Night

Chasin' It

To place an order, visit us on the web:Http:/<u>amazon.com/author/e.scrill</u>

Holy Fucking Secrets

Chapter 1

Boomer, born, Ronell J. Thomas, broke all kinds of traffic laws driving through Rouge Park-- swerving from one lane to the next at sixty miles an hour. He was trying to get to his baby momma's house in East English Village, near the ritzy Grosse Pointe Farms. He'd called her ten times.

Hola! ¿Como estas? You have reached Samara Chavez. Please leave a detailed message after the beep and I will return your call at my earliest convenience.

Remember, the most high loves
saints and sinners. Be blessed.

"Samara, why is your phone going straight
to voicemail? Call me back. RÁPIDA! Quick!" he
yelled. She knew he hated leaving voice messages.
He didn't leave them often, and when he did, it was
an indicator there was a problem. And problems
they were about to have.

*What the fuck is she doing that she got her
fucking phone off? This is unlike Samara. She
always answers for me. She never turns her phone
off,* he thought. *I want to talk to my son.* "Bitch!"
he cursed to himself, throwing his phone into the
passenger seat.

Boomer's anger with Samara eased as
semen seeped out of his flaccid dick, reminding him
of how Sister Myra deep-throated him just thirty
minutes prior.

"Swallow this dick. Use all of your mouth,"
Boomer demanded shoving her head on his rod.

"Like this?" she asked, choking, barely able
the clear his rigid nine inches.

"No! Deeper!" He thrust forcefully,
causing her to gag. "You know how I like it--nice
and sloppy!"

Sister Myra, hacked up all the saliva she could muster and spit on the reverend's piece in preparation to give him what he wanted.

They were supposed to be counting the money from the collection plates. However, the only thing Boomer counted was how many times the head of his dick hit the back of Sister Myra's throat before the sticky white substance excreted all over her heavily made up face.

*   *   *

It was times like this that Samara felt Boomer's absence the most. She wasn't the combative type. She never told him how lonely or horny she was while he was away on his business/missionary trips, fearing that it would cause an argument. So, she made due, occupying her time and satisfying her needs by alternate means. She missed him calling her his sexy, Afro-Cuban princess, looking down at her passionately with his green eyes as he slowly thrust in and out of her until they both exploded in an orgasmic euphoria. The mere thought of Boomer caused her pussy to pulsate. With each beat, her clit touched her lace thongs, arousing her internally. Samara wanted nothing more than to be doing kinky things;

she longed for her man. But, at that moment, she needed him for more than sex.

```
"Hello.  Thank you for
calling 24-hour roadside
assistance.  Press 1 for..."
```

Samara waited to hear the prompt for towing before pressing any numbers. Once she made her selection, the customer service representative appeared on the line immediately.

```
"Hello.  My name is Philando
Castile; ID 342.  Who do I have
the pleasure of assisting today?"
```

"Hi, I'm Samara Chavez. Membership number: 90919C. I'm stuck on the shoulder of the eastbound Reuther Freeway at the Gratiot exit. My transmission powered down while I was driving. I need a tow, please." Samara sunk down in her seat and tried to call Boomer...with no success. *Just great, he must still be in Antigua,* she thought, frustrated.

Before she could throw herself a mini pity-party, the tow truck driver arrived.

Scared of the speeding oncoming traffic, Samara climbed over to the passenger side and exited the vehicle. Startled when she looked up, she saw a petite, feminine woman in a flowing maxi-dress, standing at her car door.

"Oh, hi. Where is the tow truck driver?" Samara asked incredulously.

"I *am* the tow truck driver, Ms....?"

"Ms. Chavez," Samara finished, handing the driver her membership card. *A woman tow truck driver? What is her little haut self doing towing anything? In a dress at that,* Samara wondered, inconspicuously checking out the drivers stacked body.

"I'm Dominique. A few of our drivers called in, so I'll be assisting you today. Where would you like your vehicle towed to?"

"Bob Maxey Lincoln on Mack and Cadieux, please."

"No problem," Dominique smiled. "You have the premiere membership so there won't be a charge for you today. I'll wait for you to get whatever you need out of your vehicle and I will put it on the truck and we can be on our way."

The twenty minute drive to the dealership seemed like hours. Samara was put off when she tried to make small talk with the driver. Dominique was professional, but stoic. A drastic change from twenty minutes ago. *At least she could put on some music instead of making me listen to Newsradio 950 AM. This is what I get for being lazy and not charging my headset,* Samara sighed to herself, removing any hope that she and Dominique may extend communication beyond the service call.

When they finally made it to the service department at the dealership, Dominique handed Samara her business card. Co-owner, it read. Samara, confused about Dominique's flip-flopping demeanor, reached in her purse for her card holder and gave Dominique one of her business cards.

"So, you're a first lady of a church and a certified accountant, huh? A woman after my own heart."

Samara took her opportunity to be professional. "Yes, I'm everything the card states. If you ever need an accountant or a church home, call me. Have a good day, Dominique," Samara smiled, leaving the tow truck driver on the sidewalk as she walked into the dealership.

Samara went to the office of her car salesman only to find an unfamiliar woman, along with her nameplate at his desk. "Hello, I was looking for Bradley Bryan."

"Bradley is on vacation this month, and next. Is there something I can help you with?"

Samara was little apprehensive about dealing with someone new, but she knew that she couldn't wait for Bradley to return. "Ummm, well, my transmission went out on me this morning and my lease is almost up on my Lincoln MKX. I'm in the market for another vehicle."

"I'm Rainya Toussaint, and I'd be happy to help you," the melanin-rich woman said, reaching to shake Samara's hand.

Samara was caught off-guard from the jolt of energy transferred from Rainya's fingers.

"Do you have a particular model in mind you'd like to know more about or test drive?" Rainya asked, breaking Samara's daydream.

"Oh. Ah. Yes," Samara answered almost before Rainya could finish speaking. "I've had my eye on the Navigator for a while now. Specifically the tan colored one."

"Oh, yes, excellent choice!" Rainya exclaimed, oblivious to the lustful attention Samara paid to her breast. "Dune is what Lincoln calls the color, " she said, pulling the Navigator catalog out to give to Samara. "It's a beauty, inside and out."

So are you, Samara flirted with the saleswoman in her mind, imagining the softness of Rainya's perfectly heart-shaped lips. She wanted to kiss them. She wanted their tongues to dance together until both their lips went numb.

"I'll just need a copy of your identification and insurance, and we can go for a quick test drive," Rainya said, breaking Samara from her fantasy.

Rainya subtly rubbed Samara's hand as she accepted the requested documents, sending another jolt through Samara, causing her to moan slightly.

Samara and Rainya paused, looking at each other, trying to figure out what the other was thinking before getting into the Navigator.

Samara found the drive with Rainya much more pleasant than the one she'd just experienced with Dominique, the tow truck driver. Their conversation flowed naturally, extending beyond the bells and whistles of the truck, as if they'd been friends forever.

"Well, what do you think?" Rainya asked as they parked in the dealer lot. "Are you going to purchase?"

"Do you come with the purchase?" Samara asked with a sly smirk. "I definitely want you. I apologize. I definitely want the truck, but I need to speak to my significant other first," Samara answered, climbing out of the vehicle, a little embarrassed by her outburst.

She went back and forth with herself on whether or not she should wait to get Boomer's permission before doing an early lease turn-ahead and purchasing the seventy-three thousand dollar SUV. This changed however, when the charming Rainya Toussaint, hyped her up, convincing her to throw caution to the wind.

"Ms. Chavez, I don't mean to pressure you, but my records show you've been a loyal customer to Bob Maxey Lincoln, and today is the last day for the Red Carpet Lease special for returning customers. You'll lose your five thousand dollars in customer cash if you don't purchase today. Not to mention, this is the last dune colored navigator we have in stock. We don't have dune on the list of our incoming inventory." Winking at Samara, "You know what they say, 'You only live once'." She winked. "You look good in this model--much better than the black one. This color compliments you. Go ahead and splurge," Rainya urged while sneaking a glance at Samara's shapely ass. Lightly slapping Samara's arm in laughter--moving closer to her ear, in a sultry whisper, "I'll give you three business days to return the truck if Mr. Thomas doesn't approve."

Samara got the feeling the sales woman was trying to get more than a sale from her. Blushing, Samara finally conceded, "I don't see why I shouldn't indulge," referring to both the Navigator, and Rainya.

Licking her lips, Samara drove off the lot in her brand new Lincoln Navigator with an immaculate cream interior, and custom European grill. But that's not all the attention-starved, sex-deprived Samara departed the Bob Maxey dealership with.

Chapter 2

The warm wind blew in his face, calming him as he accelerated to the deep east side of Detroit in his tricked-out, pearl-iridescent, 1983 Cadillac Fleetwood Brougham. Boomer affectionately called this particular vehicle his "holy church-going car" 'cause he only drove it on Wednesdays and Sundays.

Despite having been orally satisfied by Sister Myra, Boomer's twisted mind had him envisioning the worst about Samara. *That bitch is probably laid up, letting some otha nigga sniff my sweet pussy. Or worse, she's taking some random dude into her mouth, twisting his shaft with her fingers, flicking her tongue over his head. Damn, I shouldn't have taught her that shit. I'm going to spank her ass, the first chance I get--if I don't kill her ass first,* he thought. The latter, was highly likely depending on her excuse for having her phone off.

Not once did Boomer reason that something could be wrong with Samara or their seven year old son. Nor did he take into consideration the possibility his family missed him. He'd been missing in action for over a month.

His prolonged absence was nothing out of the ordinary. After fifteen years of being in each others lives, Boomer thought Samara would be used to his disappearing acts.

Samara met Boomer while he was hustling. It was embedded in his DNA. Hustling was the only way of life he knew. Hell, it was the only life he wanted to know. Although she begged him over the years to explore other avenues, her pleas were futile.

Despite being obsessed with Samara, Boomer stood firm in his convictions; either she get with his program, or get the fuck on--her choice. And although he gave her the option to leave, the same didn't apply to his son. He made it clear, if she chose to flee, she would have to leave his son behind. Between him and his family, the boy would be just fine. He was comfortable with his lifestyle, and wasn't no bitch, nor nigga, or Holy Spirit gonna change that. He was living the dream.

*   *   *

"Have fun with your God-mommy, Kayon," Samara said, kissing her son goodbye for the evening.

"Thank you for keeping him tonight, bf. I really need some adult fun," Samara said with a grin.

"It's been a while since I've seen you make that sinister face." Not wanting her God-son or daughters to hear the conversation, Yvette told them, "Kayon, Nicolette, and, Victoria, go outside in the backyard and play on the playscape, and stay away from the pool. I'm watching y'all." As soon as they were out of earshot, Yvette sat on the bar stool facing her friend. "I can only imagine what you're about to get into, but I'm glad you're going to get out instead of being cooped up in this house."

"Who said I was going out?" Samara asked sarcastically. "I'm going to have take-out," she stated, using their code word for in-house freaking.

"Puta, what, or should I say who, is on the menu? Boomer is out of town. I know you ain't about to have another dude up in his shit!" Leaning back in her chair, Yvette paused. "Wait! Boomer is still the only guy you've been with, right?"

Samara snickered, vaguely answering Yvette's questions, not wanting to divulge who she was hooking up with. "Bf, chill. There is a first time for everything, and like you said, he ain't here, and he ain't comin' home no time soon! This is my home; whether he bought it or not."

"Okay," Yvette said throwing up her hands in peace. "I see you, but you're awfully brave all of a sudden, chica. Just be careful--please! You know Boomer's ass will have one of his rogue ass flunkies kill you and then give the eulogy at your funeral," Yvette petitioned, genuinely concerned about what she thought was an abrupt change in her friend's behavior.

* * *

Growing up, Boomer watched his paternal grandfather run numbers while his grandmother made her life living, scheming and scamming the welfare system. He learned firsthand how the pimp game worked thanks to his uncles who operated a chain of urban bordellos, employing women from all over the world, and serving men and women with every fetish and fantasy imaginable. He was most dazzled by his mother and father who ran marijuana plantations and dispensaries from one side of Eight Mile Road to the next--even before they became legal. He was intrigued and heavily influenced by his family's status as major players in the underground world of their city, despite the grime and risk that came with it.

He remembered getting a '*C*' on his fifth grade career goal essay. He wrote in great detail how he wanted to be a hustla when he grew up--like the rest of his family, including his grandparents.

"I spent a lot of time on my work. Why'd you give me a '*C*'?" he asked the teacher, balling up the paper to throw it in the trash.

Not able to relate to Boomer's homelife, his teacher did what she thought was in the best interest of his future; she tried to discourage his street dreams.

"Good morning saints. To God be the glory! Let us praise Him for waking us up and bringing us together to fellowship for yet another glorious, Sunday at Hood Hope Tabernacle.

Although I'm happy to see the pews full to capacity today, I have to tell y'all, I'm disappointed. The past few weeks, our offering plates have been on the light side. So, as to remind you all of the importance of true devotion to this church, and more importantly, to the Lord, today's sermon is about giving, sharing, and being selfless of thy self. It's better to give than to receive. Let the church say, amen! So, give of thy self and you will be rewarded abundantly. I don't hear y'all! Saints, you all are quiet today. Praise Him! Can I get an amen? Now I hear y'all! Hallelujah! Praise God. Now, please turn your Bibles to Hebrews, chapter 13, verse 16…"

The sudden halt to traffic on I-94 pulled Boomer from his thoughts of the past, back to the present. He snickered, wondering if his old English teacher, Mrs. Copin, would be proud to know he did exactly what she said he couldn't. He wrote himself a mental note to send her an invite to the annual revival next month. He wanted her to witness for herself, that despite her nay-saying, he had a successful career in hustling. All in the name of the Lord.

Boomer became a preacher to the hood; one of the most recognized in the city of Detroit, with several more money making congregations in the Midwest, and the South.

Feeding the "word" to hungry people came natural to Boomer. They wanted to believe in something and he gave them something to believe in. On many occasions, he would secretly dip into lonely and vulnerable congregants' beds, helping himself by inserting his schlong into their tight, moist, offering plates--a win-win for all those involved. He thought of his bedroom romances as another part of his service to the community. Busting a nut here and there was a perk of the job, like fringe benefits in the corporate world. It wasn't his fault folks didn't research credentials or take the time to find out who he was before accepting him as their spiritual leader.

Chapter 3

Samara, a product of rape, never knew what it was like to have a daddy. The closest thing to her having one was Boomer. He certainly was her savior. He took good care of her; just as he vowed he would after saving her from a life of lying on her back for a dollar. So, when he did his thing, she knew what it was. For the most part, he was an open book as far as she was concerned. She knew what he was doing and in some cases, who he was doing it with. She was well aware his line of work took him away for days at a time. But she also knew that like dogs, he always found his way back home.

Mariposa Antonia, the woman who gave birth to her, was not even half of a mother to

Samara or her younger siblings. Always cruel and drugged out, Mariposa resented Samara and never made her feelings a secret. She'd always tell Samara how much she hated her. In Samara's senior year of high school, Mariposa showed just how deep-rooted her hate for Samara ran. Instead of celebrating her sweet sixteen birthday with a party like most teenage girls, Samara's mother tried to sell her to Boomer's uncles, The Three Horsemen, for a measly week's supply of heroin. Mariposa was more concerned that she and her man of the month get high, than the well-being and happiness of her daughter. Mariposa was well aware of the reputation of The Three Horsemen, as they were notoriously known in the underworld of the city; one, for their massive manly endowments, as well as for the way they rode the shit out of their whores, ensuring they brought home every dollar earned, to the Horsemen enterprise.

"Wake up, Samara. Hurry up and get dressed! Your clothes are on the sink. When you get done, come to my bedroom so I can make up your face."

Samara went into the rundown bathroom expecting to see the big, pretty, yellow dress she showed her mother at the mall a week earlier. She was excited, thinking her mother was taking her somewhere special for her sixteenth birthday. Her excitement vanished and horror set in when she saw a pair of lace thongs placed on top of a short, bordello-red, bodycon dress, draped over the crumbling vanity.

Before Samara could cry in protest, her mother burst into the bathroom. "Puta, what the fuck are you doing? Why aren't you getting dressed?"

With tears forming in her eyes, Samara spoke at a whisper. "Madre, I don't want to wear that. I don't even know how to walk in heels, and won't those panties go in my butt?"

Clenching her teeth, she tightly grabbed Samara's wrist, holding them down to her sides. "Put the fucking clothes on! Prisa; ahora mismo! Now!" she demanded. "We are going to be late for our appointment."

The last thing Boomer expected to see on his weekly cash drop to his uncles' whorehouse in The District was Mariposa and her oldest daughter. The mother walked with determination, dragging her daughter into the underground utopia his family lobbied for, financed and developed. The tunnel that ran the length and width of the city, comprised of all the city's sanctioned liquor stores, dispensaries, casinos, whorehouses and strip clubs.

"What are they doing here?" He looked to
his uncles for answers, but they all shrugged, just as
confused as Boomer. They weren't expecting them,
and underage girls were not a part of their normal
business practices.

Boomer thought Mariposa was a recovering
junkie because he'd seen her attending the Narcotics
Anonymous meetings held at his southwest church
campus. She, like his other congregants, didn't
have a clue about his affiliation with this part of his
life. And he intended to keep it that way. Before
she or her daughter could see him, he moved to a
back room and watched behind the two-way mirror.
He listened intently as Mariposa gave what sounded
like a rehearsed sales pitch.

"She is legal now; she can consent to sex,"
as if she had previously discussed with The
Horsemen the sale of her daughter, but they
declined due to her age.

"I guarantee, she'll make y'all a fortune,"
Mariposa pleaded, spinning Samara around, giving
the men full view of her body. "She won't be the
streetwalker kind, either. You can sell her to your
upscale customers--your politicians and
businessmen," she said with desperation. "I know
she'll make one a hell of an escort. Think about
your customers who have a thing for young virgins.

Bid her to the highest bidder. I'm telling you, she is smart," Mariposa bragged. "This girl here ain't no dummy. She does math in her head faster than you can give her the math problem. She has a photogenic memory and can remember anything you place in front of her. Plus, she can cook her ass off. She makes three different cuisines: Cuban, American and Thai. And she keeps house good, too. Did I mention she is quiet. She don't speak, unless you speak to her."

Everyone in the room looked over at the teary-eyed Samara who hadn't said one word in protest of what her mother was doing.

Twenty-one year-old Boomer listened intentionally from the time the mother and daughter stepped foot into the building. He was glad he was present on this day, hearing everything the girl's mother said, trying to convince his uncles to purchase her. He was captivated by Samara's flawless skin. She was a redbone with thick, jet-black hair that hung past her ass. He wanted this beauty for himself.

No longer concerned about his identity being exposed, Boomer stormed out of the back room, interrupting the negotiations, making an offer to the girl's mother and his uncles. "I want her." Looking the mother in the eye. "I'll give you a month's supply of brown. But, do not come around here or the church, and do not contact your daughter ever again. Do you understand?" Boomer asked through his gritted teeth. He could see the greed in Mariposa's eyes. It was obvious to him she was more than happy with his offer.

"Yes, I understand. And you don't have to worry. I'm happy to be rid of this little cunt-bitch!" Rubbing her tracked up hands together, she spoke with excitement, "You got yourself a deal, young man!"

Turning to face his uncles, Boomer offered all the spare cash he had on him. "I will give you seventy-five thousand for her. That's twenty-five thousand--cash, for each of you."

The uncles appeared hesitant to accept their only nephew's offer. They knew if the girl was in fact a virgin, she was worth way more than what Boomer put on the table. Besides the monetary value, they could expand their business to regions they hadn't been able to break into in the past. Acquiring her would strengthen their protection against arrest, prosecution and much more.

The oldest of the three uncles began with, "Nephew, I speak for all of us when I say the virgin holds way more value than what you're offering. I have a client that has a fetish for virgins. His demand is greater than the supply. I know he would pay at least a half-million, if not more, to have her as his mistress in some foreign land. The same politician would open doors outside of our current borders. He has connections in Las Vegas and New York City. This is big for business, Boomer."

Boomer wanted what he wanted, and was not trying to hear what his uncle was proposing. He knew none of his uncles would challenge him because they would have to answer to his father, and that is something they just wouldn't do.

With his fist balled to his sides, Boomer made it clear he was not going to accept no for an answer. "Find another virgin. This one is mine!"

Boomer's youngest and favorite uncle spoke up. "Man, let him have the young bitch." Focusing his attention to Boomer. "But, you will find two more virgins to replace this one. And, you got a week to do it, or the deal is off. Don't fuck her until you make good on your end. You understand, nephew?" his uncle asked, eyeing him sternly.

"Unc, you don't even have to worry. I'm not touching her until she turns eighteen. As far as your virgins, the church is full of them. I'll bring you a flock," he responded sarcastically.

Boomer had never overlapped his religious endeavors and his family business in this manner in the three years he'd been ministering in the church, but somehow he knew saving Samara from his uncles would be worth it. His role in the church was better played with a leading lady, and now, he had her. He would have to groom her for a couple of years and when the time was right, he would present her to each of his congregations as his bride and First Lady of Hood Hope Tabernacle.

Mariposa forcefully nudged Samara in her back, ushering her towards Boomer. "Go on now, chica."

Despite the uncomfortable platform heels that adorned her feet, Samara was firmly planted. She didn't budge.

Boomer put his hand up, signaling Mariposa to stop. He walked over to Samara and placed his shirt over her scantily dressed body. Besides not appreciating seeing young girls dressed like prostitutes, Samara, was shivering. He could hear her teeth chattering from the cold or fear, or both.

"Thank you," Samara murmured.

Wiping her tear-stained face, Boomer reassured her, "It's going to be okay. I promise." He gently took her hand in his as he looked her up

and down, inspecting her. "We need to get you
some new 'fits. Maybe take you to get your hair
done, too," he suggested as he rubbed his hand
through her silky mane.

Samara winced at his touch, muttering,
"Okay," and not saying anything more, looking
down at the stained cement floors to avoid all the
staring eyes in the room.

Trying not to be a bad sport about his loss,
the oldest uncle interrupted Boomer's inspection of
Samara with, "Where is our seventy-five thousand
dollars, nephew?"

Samara's mother took the opportunity to
casually remind Boomer what she was promised.
"I'll just take my fix and be on my way."

Chapter 4

Although Boomer promised himself and his uncles that he wouldn't touch her until she turned eighteen, Samara wanted so badly to feel him inside of her. She would've settled for his hands meeting her skin in a sensual way on the surface of her body, but he didn't pay her any attention in that way. He treated her more like a little sister. Boomer stayed on her about her grades; showing up for her parent-teacher conferences, talking to her about envious bitches, teaching her how to handle them. He even showed her how to fix a flat and change her own motor oil.

Samara only began to notice her physical attraction for him after living with him for a year, when she mistakenly walked in on him one morning, getting out of the shower.

"Oh my, God! I'm sorry! I didn't know you were in my bathroom. I thought you'd be in yours," Samara screamed, pulling the door closed as she ran out of the bathroom with her head down in embarrassment.

Boomer snatched the frilly shower curtain, covering himself. "My shower heads aren't working. The plumber can't replace them until tomorrow," he shouted through the closed door.

For the next few days, Samara played it off, pretending she didn't see his erect manhood. But, she couldn't deny to her seventeen-and-a-half year-old body that she was aroused by seeing his muscular body and curved piece hanging low between his bowlegs, inciting her pussy to dance involuntarily. Samara fantasized about him at night before bed, leaving her with little choice but to masturbate as she fantasized about how one day he would be all hers. She couldn't wait for the day she wouldn't have to share his 5 feet--10 inches, red hair and dimples with those chicks that came in and out of their condo like a revolving door night after night.

Boomer didn't think Samara was aware of his trysts, but she was. And although she never saw the women, she heard them as he pleasured them, making them scream, always begging for more.

Excited about her play date, Samara tried on teddy after teddy from her lingerie closet. After finally settling on a metal, chain-embellished, Hidden Pleasures Intimates babydoll, she slipped on her turquoise platforms, lacing them up to her thick thighs. She fondled herself in her floor-to-ceiling mirror, pinching her nipples and then rubbing them for comfort. *Not bad for 31 years old. I look just as good, if not better than I did at sixteen.*

She was ready to grab one of her many glass dildos to give herself a quick selfie when a bell rung, alerting her that someone had pulled into her driveway, putting a halt to her plans. *It's early. I'm not expecting company for another twenty minutes.*

Samara watched through the camera monitor, admiring her guest of the evening strut up the winding walkway to the front door. She didn't want to seem too anxious so she didn't open the door until the doorbell rang.

"Hello, mamacita," her guest said, handing her a bouquet of hot-pink roses.

"These are beautiful! Thank you!" Samara exclaimed, holding the flowers with one hand, firmly hugging her date with the other, sneaking a kiss on the cheek with the embrace.

Her guest moved closer into the embrace, sniffing Samara's neck. "You smell good enough to eat. What do you have on?"

"Pink Sugar," Samara answered, licking her full, naked lips.

"I hope you taste as good as you look and smell, Suga. Are you addictive like sugar?" her guest inquired.

Samara grinned, "Now that, you'll have to find out for yourself," placing her index finger in her mouth, twirling her tongue around her finger as if it were a sucker.

"You're a little early and I'm not quite ready, but come in and have a seat in the den while I finish getting myself together. Can I get you something to drink? The bar is fully stocked."

"No," her date replied. "I want to enjoy you, sound mind and sober."

Blushing, Samara countered with, "I can make you a mocktail. It will taste just as good. You're going to need to be hydrated for what we're about to do, baby."

"I'll take a mocktail then--something with pineapple juice," her guest conceded.

"One mocktail with pineapple juice coming right up!"

*   *   *

His police radar was on the fritz. It seemed that traffic enforcement had speed traps set up throughout the city, slowing him down significantly. Had it not been for the wild turkey walking out in front of his car on Tireman and Outer Drive, Boomer would've been pulled over and ticketed for sure. He did appreciate the scenery on his drive. The city was polluted with flowers and mature trees. Most of the dilapidated buildings that once plagued the city had been demolished and replaced with community gardens. The air had a sweet, fragrant smell. Kind of like...Samara.

Man who am I fooling? I miss my bitch. My first lady." Boomer retrieved his phone from the passenger seat, making one last attempt to reach Samara. Still, his calls were going straight to voicemail.

Boomer realized his life calling and personal contribution to the family business would be preaching at the ripe age of eighteen when he did a short stint in Wayne County's Dickerson Facility in Hamtramck, Michigan.

When Boomer turned onto his street, he immediately saw two unfamiliar vehicles in his driveway. His stomach began to turn, his heart raced, and his palms became a clammy. *Who's Navigator is this and where is Samara's truck?* he thought. He walked in the backyard hoping to see his son swimming in the pool. When he didn't see his boy in the pool he checked the lavish tree house. Boomer soon realized his son wasn't outside and made his way to the side of the house where he heard pounding and knocking inside the brick home. He moved closer to the house, putting his ear to the door. Thunderous moaning added to the knocking and pounding. *I gotta be tripping 'cause I know this bitch don't have no nigga in here, fucking around my son!*

Hearing the unmistakable sound of a headboard banging against a wall, his blood boiled. *This slut* is *giving my pussy away!* He quietly eased his key into the door, letting himself in.

Boomer walked lightly through the house, following the sounds of passion coming from the rear of the oversized bungalow he purchased when Samara gave birth to his firstborn, Kayon. What

Boomer saw when he got to the biggest of the two first-floor bedrooms gave him pause.

"Holy fuckin' secrets! This is why my calls were going straight to voicemail," he muttered.

There was a fine, deep, dark broad in the California king-sized bed he shared with Samara. His manhood jumped in his pants at the sight of the strange woman's legs spread wide, held by chains suspended from the vaulted ceiling. Samara was fucking the woman with a strap-on. The leather strips attaching it tightly hugged Samara's plump ass, making it jiggle as she thrust in and out of the woman's pussy with long, slow strokes. She was so wet that he could hear each stroke above her moans for more. His dick became rock-like, erecting a tent in his dress slacks. His emotions went from angry to confused, to devilishly aroused.

Samara and her lover were so into each other that they were oblivious to Boomer's presence. For what seemed like forever, he stood off to the side of the doorway. To please himself, he spit on his hand and stroked his dick as he watched the women from the wall-covered mirror in the hallway. Boomer didn't have a clue that Samara was into the ladies. Had he known, she could've helped him bed down women a long time ago. Not that he needed assistance, but having multiple beautiful women together--at the same damn time, was always a plus in his book.

He must've made a noise stroking himself because Samara looked up. Their eyes met in the mirror.

Busted! Boomer thought.

Samara didn't stop pleasing her lover at the sight of Boomer. Instead, she motioned with her pointy finger, inviting him to join in. Samara pulled back, removing the oversized, silicone dildo from her lover's pussy. She re-positioned herself on all fours--her ass kissed the air, and her face replaced the faux dick that was previously inside her lover.

Boomer spread Samara's ass, sliding all nine inches of his dick into Samara's throbbing, moistened pussy. He almost came. "Your tight-ass pussy is squeezing my dick!" he yelled, excitedly. "Stop! Get on top!"

Samara did as she was told and mounted Boomer, giving him more control.

Just when he didn't think he could get any harder, Boomer grew stiffer as he watched Samara's large, brown nipples bounce in his face as she sensually moved up and down his pole, opening and closing her pussy as Rainya caressed Boomer's balls with her tongue.

"Choke me, daddy. Please!"

He knew what this meant so he wrapped both his hands around her neck, squeezing with light force.

"Daddy, I'm about--I'm about to cum all over your dick," Samara panted. "I'm tapping out." She kissed Rainya's ear with, "You wanna give my daddy some of your sweet pussy, baby?"

Rainya, moaned, "Yes. Let me feel him."

Samara leaned against the pole at the foot of the bed, masturbating as she watched Boomer please Rainya with fast, hard strokes. The louder Rainya shouted in pleasure, the harder Samara rubbed herself, bringing on an intense orgasm.

Samara, Rainya and Boomer spooned until Samara got restless.

"How about the three of us take a shower, and then I'll make us some of my famous French toast and scrambled eggs?" Samara offered.

"Sounds good to me. You two helped me work up an appetite," Boomer answered, rubbing his belly.

Rainya kissed Samara on the back of her neck and told her, "Sure, baby, anything you want."

The familiarity in which Samara and Rainya spoke to each other made Boomer wonder how long they'd been dealing with each other. He would speak to Samara about it later. For now, he wanted to enjoy whatever the two women were providing.

Boomer slid the patio door open, ushering Samara and Rainya through. Samara grabbed both Boomer and Rainya's hands, leading them to the hidden outdoor shower.

Rainya was impressed with the design and functionality. "This is so nice!" she exclaimed. "Maybe we should chill in the hot tub instead of having breakfast."

"How about we have breakfast inside the hot tub?" Samara suggested.

Boomer frowned with, "I don't think that would be a good idea. We can eat and then chill in the hot tub."

Not wanting to challenge Boomer, Samara lathered a new loofah with body wash and began to rub Rainya down, kissing her body along the way.

Rainya returned the favor while Boomer observed on the shower bench, waiting for his turn

when Rainya pulled him up so that he was
positioned between her and Samara.

"You don't get to watch and not work, sir,"
Rainya said playfully.

Boomer licked his upper lip. "I've never
been scared of work, baby." Using both of his
hands to wash each woman he continued with,
"Turn around, Rainya, let me get your front."

As soon as Rainya turned to face him, she
recalled where she'd seen him. "I knew you looked
familiar. You're the preacher with the billboards on
the freeways." She smirked at the realization of
what she'd done. "I've never sexed a member of
the clergy before. But don't worry, this is our
secret. Shoot, I want to be invited to come back for
second helpings," Rainya confessed.

"Oh, you'll definitely be invited back for
more," Samara said, massaging Rainya's spine with
the balls of her fingers.

"In fact, why don't you come to church?
We're having our annual revival next month at
Cobo Hall. Bring a friend," Boomer encouraged,
never missing an opportunity to grow his
congregation.

"I was going to ask if you were interested in serving on our usher board," Samara whispered in Rainya's ear while twirling her hair around her fingers.

"Sounds like you both want me to stick around," Rainya said, blushing.

"We do!" Samara and Boomer said in unison.

Both Samara and Boomer hated that their time with Rainya had come to an end. They walked her to her truck and said their goodbyes with more fondling and kissing, promising to hook up again soon. They watched as she pulled off and headed back into the house.

"Meet me in the spare room, Samara," Boomer sternly demanded. "It's unlocked."

Samara walked in the room to "Gett Off" by Prince playing. She pranced over to sit in the matching chair next to Boomer.

"Naw," he said firmly, shaking his head. "Don't sit. Stand," he commanded. "Give me your hands."

She did as she was told, holding her arms out in front of her.

"Is that too tight?" he asked, placing her wrists one-by-one in the wide, leather arm cuffs attached to suspension chains that hung from the ceiling.

"A little," she whimpered seductively.

"That's it, my sweets?" he asked, biting his bottom lip. "A little? How about this?" He penetrated her eyes with his, firmly yanking the pull chain that adorned her neck, drawing her to the floor.

She landed in a kneeling position, her face almost touching his hardened manhood. The sub was tempted to free her tongue from her moist mouth to lick her master, but she knew the consequences of acting on her own accord. She yearned for him to give her permission to touch him, but he was taking his sweet time. It had been too long and she ached to feel him.

"Mansa, can I please…?"

"Shuuuuuuush!" He put his pointy finger to his full, heart-shaped lips, silencing her. "Sweets, did I tell you to speak?"

"No, Mansa." She looked up at his inviting eyes.

"Did I even ask you a question?" he snarled, twisting his lips up.

Keeping her eyes aligned with his, she whispered, "No, Mansa." She was sure her speaking out of turn would delay the pleasure she badly anticipated.

"Lie back. Spread your legs. I want to smell you." He took a long whiff, inhaling her essence. "Your scent is intoxicating. I'm going to figure out how to bottle your fragrance and take it with me," he whispered, rubbing his face against her bare pussy. "Mmmmm, your skin is so soft," he said tickling the inside of her thighs with his fingers.

She giggled.

"Turn on your stomach." He replaced his fingers with a leather flogger, caressing the length of her body before striking her backside. "Does this feel good, my sweets?"

Moans of painful pleasure seeped from her lips, "Ohhh ahhh, Mansa. More. I need more," she pleaded as her body jerked.

"I see you can't be still. I got something for that." Boomer pulled the plastic wrap from under the bed, wrapping Samara's body, leaving only her

90

head and nipples exposed. He reached into the mini refrigerator and pulled out the nipple clamps. "You've been a bad girl. And you know what happens to bad girls, right?" he asked smiling, exposing his teeth.

Her face lit up as he pinched her nipples, readying them for what was to come. "It means I have to wear cold nipple clamps."

"Correct, sweets," he said, placing the clamps on her erect nipples.

Boomer wanted to tease Samara a while longer. He mind-fucked her for as long as he could stand, giving her nothing but silent stares. His objective was to see how long she could sustain before begging to be touched. Each time, her stamina grew.

Ready to grant her desires, he asked, "Where's the cat o' nine tails?" as he searched the toy vault.

"It's in the back of the vault," she pointed with her head. "Daddy, what did I do? Why are you going to spank me?" she whined, feigning fear of being punished physically. It was all a part of their game.

"Slut, I'm asking the fucking questions. Understand?" He cuffed Samara's small chin in his hand, kissing her forcefully.

"Yes."

"Yes, who?"

"Yes, daddy." His abrasive kissing was her signal that his role was switching from Mansa to daddy.

"That's better," Boomer offered, stroking her damp hair. "Now, how hard daddy spanks you will depend on how you answer my questions. You understand, my love?"

"Yes, daddy."

"That's daddy's good girl," he announced, lightly biting Samara's shoulder.

"So, am I the only man that has felt the inside of you?"

"Yes, daddy," Samara answered, her eyes begging him to believe her.

Boomer knew she was being honest so he tapped her with the leather vigorously the way she liked it. "You and Rainya seem like you been grinding on each other for a while. How long y'all been hooking up?" Boomer asked.

"Tonight was our first time. I bought the Navigator from her today."

"You sure?" he asked, slipping his hand around her throat.

"I'm sure, daddy," she answered, barely audible.

"How long you been sharing my pussy?"

"I've been--I've been playing with girls for a while. Remember when I was just 17 and you wouldn't touch me?"

Boomer nodded.

"I have one more question." Boomer stood directly in front of Samara, sweat dripping from his muscular pecs.

"Yes, daddy," Samara moaned.

"Samara Chavez, will you marry me?"

END

Fauzykiss is a Detroit native and the author of The Erogenous Confessions anthology. An avid reader, she unabashedly admits, reading is her drug of choice. Adding, she derives gratification by sharing in her love of reading by hooking reluctant readers.

Fauzykiss is currently working on, "From His Wife to His Sidepeice," an erotic suspense, under the Shenomenal Ink imprint.

Thank you for reading.

Connect with Fauzykiss at:

Facebook: @fauzykissthewriter

Instagram: @fauzykiss

Twitter: @fauzykiss

Erogenous Confessions is available at:

www.amazon.com

www.barnesandnoble.com

Apple-iBooks

Who's The Boss?

The Boss

As I stand here pinned against the wall with this nigga's hand around my neck, I had to bite my lip to keep from laughing in his face. *He really thinks he's the one in control.*

"Did you hear what the fuck I said?"

His emphasis on the word "*fuck*" snapped me back out of my head because that's all I really wanted to do.

"I heard you," I said timidly.

"Let me have to repeat myself again."

"And then, what?"

"You and that smart ass mouth…" he said as he closed his fingers tighter, cutting off a bit of my air.

My eyes rolled back, not because I was about to pass out, but because I was about to cum.

"Yo' ass likes that shit, don't you?" he asked, shaking his head.

The corners of my mouth must have curled a little too much. I guess I wasn't doing too good of a job holding in that smile.

I said nothing, just looked in his eyes. He closed his, took a deep breath, and loosened his grip slightly before covering my lips with his and said, "I love your crazy ass."

My response was the way I welcomed his tongue; how I feverishly cupped the sides of his face like I'd been waiting on that kiss all my life. I had. Not all my life, but since he walked through the door. Hell, even that's a lie. I been thinking about those lips since I woke up this morning.

I inhaled his scent as I tried to breathe him in. He'd backed away slightly and was barely gripping my neck at this point. I started pushing away from the wall, attempting to walk him backwards. My hands loosened his belt and zipper. With both hands I grabbed his neck, spun him around and slammed him against that same wall. Leaning in on tipped toes, I whispered in his ear,

"When I tell you to bring me my dick, that's what the fuck I mean!"

Before he could respond, I was on my knees looking up at him, stroking his dick while my tongue massaged his balls. He peered down at me and just as he was about to speak, I wrapped my lips around that big, thick dick. Whatever words he was about to speak caught in his throat. I took every inch; wet and sloppy--slurping like my life depended on it. When he grabbed a hand full of my hair and forced his dick deeper down my throat, I almost passed out. Not because I couldn't breathe, (because I couldn't) but from the excitement. I loved when he did that shit and he knew it. The deeper he tried to get, the wetter my mouth and my pussy got. I promise, he was on the verge of making me cum.

Him first! I stepped my game up and gave good suction with my jaws, made sure my slurps were heard over the running shower that I was just about to step into when all that started. When I heard him moan, I knew it was all me. I grabbed his hips and made him fuck my face. He unloaded his hot, sweet nut down my throat about the tenth pump in. I stood slowly with a full smirk on my face as he stood, trying to catch his breath. I didn't say one word. The shower was beckoning for me, so I answered.

I stood, letting the hot water soothe me, pleased with myself for showing him who was truly in control. When the shower door opened and closed, I didn't bother turning around. I knew it was him coming to wash me of my sins along with his. He leaned into me. I returned the gesture by leaning into his chest.

"Is that how you tell me you love me back?"

I didn't respond.

"There you go again making me repeat myself."

I hadn't planned on dignifying his statement with a response either. But, my voice was heard whether I'd been planning it or not. I couldn't hold the squeal that followed as he pressed his full rod into my ass. I hadn't paid attention to him soaping up--too wrapped up in my own celebration. He knew I wouldn't pull away, that would mean he'd won. I stood as still as I could for a moment. He slowly rocked, making sure I got every inch. And as much as I wanted to remain silent, I couldn't.

"Shiiiiiit!"

"Oh, you can speak now?"

"Yeeees," I moaned.

"I said, 'don't make me repeat myself'," he said to the rhythm of each thrust which had become much harder.

"Okay!"

"Okay? That's all you have to say?"

His pace and veracity had increased considerably. Now that I wanted to say something, I actually couldn't. The best I could muster were pants, moans and whimpers from the pleasure. I was now bent over, water beating on my back, streaming in my hair and face.

"You're still not answering me!" He demanded an answer.

"I forgot the question," I managed to belt out.

"Is that how you tell me you love me?"

"Yes."

"Yes, what?"

He hadn't let up, only paused every time I came which I'd managed to do at least twice in the five minutes he assaulted my ass.

"Yesssss, daddy!"

"Oh, you do remember my name? I thought you forgot."

"No, baby, no."

Fuck that, he isn't getting the best of me. I started throwing it back.

"There you go."

"That's what you want?"

"You know what I want."

We met each other thrust for thrust.

"I want that nut right there, daddy."

"Right there?"

"Yessss," I hissed.

"You asking me or telling me?"

"Please, daddy?"

"Oh, you're begging for it now?"

"Yes, daddy, please?"

"Give me what I want and maybe your greedy ass can have what you want."

"Ok, baby."

"Don't just tell me okay," he said, then started pounding me like he was a jack hammer and I was the concrete.

The water had gone cold and neither one of us cared. I knew what he wanted and I'd been purposely trying to hold on to it but it was happening no longer.

"I love you, daddddddy!" I screamed as a strong orgasm rushed through my body.

I began to shake just as his final thrust came with a deep groan that I could almost feel extend through his member. It pulsed as he shot his load in my ass. All I could do was lean against the shower wall with heavy breaths. *Shit*!

We quickly lathered up, rinsed, and then jumped from the chilled water. In his normal fashion, Marvin dried me with the fluffy bath sheet, then wrapped it around my body. I swear this man treats me like no other man has. Even when I give him reasons to walk away from me, he finds a way to let me know I mean the world to him.

Every time he does this to me, I think of when we met. I knew the moment I saw him, he would be a good lay. I thought I'd be the one giving him the business, but he surprised the hell out of me--serving up some business. That is, when I finally got him to give in.

He wouldn't give me the time of day when we first met. It took me months to get him to give up the goods. But, ba-by, when I opened up that package, it was well worth the wait. In the process of talking him out that dick, I fucked around and fell in love with his fine ass. I'd never tell him that though. I'll let him keep thinking it's a superficial love based on the sex. It'll make things messier than they already are.

Marvin made me work for it alright. His 6-foot, thin frame made him look way less menacing than he actually was. There were several reasons he tried not to get involved with me. One, namely was his lifestyle, to which, I will admit, is something foreign to me. He's what one would consider a thug. Very street, but on the surface, he looks like a well-mannered business man.

His front is real estate. That is how I wrangled him in; under the guise of purchasing a new home. I'd contacted him, telling him the things I was looking for. The next day, he sent me a list of properties fitting my parameters. The day after that, I sent him a list of the ones I wanted to view; four in total.

We met at the realtor's office, then he drove to the locations with me in tow. He tried to keep it professional, and for a house or two, I played along. When we got in that third house though, I couldn't hold it in anymore. The day was warm, almost unseasonably so for the spring. I had on a long-sleeved wrap-dress that hit my curves in all the right places. Marvin tried to pretend as if he didn't notice those curves, but I caught him gawking a few times.

Anyway, as we walked through the third house, I swayed just a little more than usual as he followed. While he meandered down the hall, he started spewing off what the property offered. I barely heard him. I was thinking about all I wanted to do to and with him. Spending time in the car with him, watching him move, listening to his everyday world, and seeing the quirks in his mannerisms made me want more of him. I wanted to devour him so I could learn him and subsequently own him.

He snapped me from my run-a-way thoughts when he said, "You'll love this room here." He passed me in the hall. "Follow me."

"There's what used to be a servants' quarters or maybe for a nanny. But a woman like you, I'm sure, can use it as a sitting room or beauty bar or perhaps...."

"A sex room," I interrupted.

His next words caught in his throat. I could tell he didn't know what to say next or even how to react. I squeezed by him in the doorway so my body grazed his, then I surveyed the room

"I was going to say walk in closet but I suppose that would work too," he finally announced.

"I can see the swing here, bench here," I said as I rounded the room.

I continued to name things I'd hang, strap or otherwise around the room, and I enjoyed seeing his cheeks turn rosy. I decided to let him off the hook. I wouldn't press him to engage any further right then. I like to play with my food before I eat. Or so I thought.

"Let's grab something to eat before the next place. I'm starved."

"Sure," he responded as he looked into my eyes.

I'd stopped right in front of him to make sure he saw my face, full and clearly. I was being straight up with him and I needed him to see that I was not ashamed or hiding from the things I was saying.

"You pick the place, any place you'd like--my treat. You can have whatever you like." I saw his eyebrow raise slightly when I said that, but I acted as if I didn't. I knew then I had him.

We had a few cocktails at dinner with some general conversation. I learned where he was from and what brought him to Las Vegas, of all places, to live. I could tell from his story he was leaving something out that he wasn't quite ready to tell me. But, I wouldn't push. People like to keep their pasts buried for a reason. The rest of the day was uneventful. I let him ponder what I'd said in the third house. After seeing the last house, we returned to the real estate office and went our separate ways.

The Chase

It took me nearly three months to find a house that I wanted to put an offer in on. Partly, because I wanted to keep feeling Marvin out. But, the one I put the offer in on was the day *he* sealed the deal.

Our routine had been the same once a week for the three months I looked. We'd meet at his office, he'd drive me place to place, we'd stop to eat, back to the office, and repeat a week later. We kept in touch via email or text in between time. I'd gotten him to loosen up a bit. And at each house we saw, I got a little flirtier; increasingly more brushes with my body and quite a bit more touchy-feely.

The last house was an adventure. It had one of those servants' quarters, but instead of presenting it to me in that manner, Marvin addressed it as I had.

"Follow me," Marvin said.

I did as he requested. We reached a room and he opened the door.

"This house has that bonus sex room like one of the earlier ones."

I stepped over the threshold. When I entered the room, I got a little shiver. It was something about the energy in the room. Visions popped into my head of all the many things I could fashion to the walls, space for benches--there were so many possibilities. I didn't verbalize any of them. Unlike the last place when I just threw the notion out, this time I felt it.

Marvin snatched me out of the thoughts I got lost in. He'd said something I hadn't heard. I turned to ask what it was and he was so very close to me our lips nearly touched. It frightened me a bit.

"I'm, I'm sorry I didn't hear you. What did you say?" I stammered.

"I said, 'you seemed to be impressed with this room'."

I hadn't moved away from him. We stood nearly nose to nose.

"This room is a great selling point."

"So, what do I need to do to seal the deal?"

I leaned into his ear.

"Show me what this room can do."

Not another word was spoken. He grabbed both my arms and pushed me back against the wall. I gasped as he forced his hand down my pants, under my panties and into my pussy in what seemed like one motion. What met his fingers was hot and wet. He'd let a moan escape his throat that let me know he was pleased. He used his fingers as if he were a pianist and my body was his piano. Marvin knew exactly what he was doing and he made sure I knew, too. I gripped his shoulders as he pleased me against that wall. My pants and moans echoed through the empty house.

Just as I was about to cum all over his hand, he stopped. Marvin still said nothing, looked into my eyes as I caught my breath and cleaned my juices from his fingers with his tongue. I wanted to taste me on him so I leaned in and kissed him. Somehow, my jeans were unbuttoned and at my ankles. He knelt in front of me with his fingers hooked at both sides of my panties. Marvin slowly slid them down while his face was so close to my crotch I could feel his breath. Just as my underwear hit the top of my pants at my ankles, I felt his mouth cover my clit. His tongue played tricks with me. Steadily, he coaxed my body into releasing. His tongue twisted and twirled and I felt every movement. He'd released one of my legs from the pool of clothing at my feet and placed it over his shoulder. His slurps and moans couldn't be heard in the echoes, drowned out by my exclamations of ecstasy. His fingers once again found their way to his piano. My body bounced up and down the wall by the pressure of his movement. My hands gripped his shoulders for balance while I looked around in disbelief of what was happening. Not because we were doing what would be considered indecent, but because I'd let him gain control. He could have it. I needed him to take control. It was the last thing I expected but it was also a refreshing change.

My moans became louder as his tongue and fingers moved faster. His hand got deeper, feeling my crevice to capacity. I shivered, my body tingled, and I felt as if a wave was rising in my body--starting from my toes. It grew stronger as it moved through my body. My moans grew louder, gearing up for my climax. I felt it coming, growing,

and rumbling through my veins. He played my
body as if it had always been his. He did not stop
until that wave became the tsunami he was calling
for. My moans had transformed into a scream and
echoed through the house as if it were a reverb
coming from a malfunctioning speaker. I felt as if I
were floating. When I came down, his dick was
waiting to replace his fingers. I was so wrapped up
in my ecstasy I hadn't seen him make a move, let
alone pull out that beast. As a matter of fact, I
didn't see it at all, I just felt it. With my mouth
agape and my eyes closed, a stifled scream caught
in my throat. It seemed as if it were stuck there.

Marvin made sure I felt every inch. He
buried himself deeply into me. He was giving me
everything I'd been fantasizing about for the last
three months. I felt that wave rising again. It was
then that he asked, "This is what you've been
wanting, isn't it?"

I couldn't manage to get a word from my
mouth. I simply moaned in agreement.

"You ever heard of 'be careful what you ask
for'?"

I came so hard listening to his baritone
voice. Every ounce of me released into the
atmosphere. I felt him pulsing inside me, letting his
own juice fill me. *How stupid is that?* When he

released me, I was relieved to see he'd had on a
condom. I'd missed that motion all together.
Thank goodness someone was being responsible.
We dressed in silence and saw no more houses that
day. He'd driven back to the office and I got in my
own vehicle and drove away without a word. The
next day, I sent him an email requesting he'd submit
my offer on that property.

We didn't see each other again until I had to
enter the office to sign my "good faith letter". I
hadn't texted, emailed or anything. I tried to tell
myself I'd gotten what I wanted and it was over.
But, when I saw him, my whole body shivered. We
avoided any prolonged eye contact and kept our
interaction short and to the point. But after
continuous debate with myself throughout the day, I
gave in. Just as I slid into bed, I sent a simple text,
then anxiously awaited a response.

It was nice seeing you today.

Half an hour went by before my phone
dinged.

You looked delicious.

That was the door that opened and a year
later it hasn't closed.

The Trap

I've tried to just back away from Marvin but something just draws me even closer. I'm intrigued by his inhibition and adventurous nature. It's like an addiction. I try to stay away from him but the more I try, the harder it gets to resist.

Once, he showed up at my son's birthday party and we ended up fucking in the bathroom. I couldn't help it, he cornered me. Just like now, he's in the den watching the football game with my husband, and I'm trying to figure out how I can suck his dick without raising suspicions.

I hate that Jason (my husband) befriended him when we bought this fucking house. Every time I walk into my private sitting room, I think of how he made me orgasm. Jason thinks I go in there for solitude, for a place away from him and the kids. I go in that room to cum over and over again at the thought of Marvin. Jason has no idea I spend my time making videos for Marvin to view. Nor does he know how to instruct me the way Marvin does to push me beyond what I thought my limits were. Jason is so one-sided, he thought me giving him a rim job was too much. While I have Marvin flirting with the idea of allowing me to massage his prostate while I give him head. I guess I'm equally addictive to him. He's so much as told me so.

Here I am playing dutiful hostess/wife, making appetizers and mixing drinks while Marvin is sitting in there laughing and making nice with his date. I don't like it in the least. You can bet he picked the church Jezebel to get under my skin. You see, that's where we met initially, in church.

Marvin doesn't really want to start playing games with me. He has no idea how truly savage I can be.

"Your home is really beautiful," Chandler (The Jezebel) said.

"Thank you. Marvin helped us find it."

"He didn't tell me that."

"Would you like a tour?" I asked.

The way Marvin bucked his eyes almost made me giggle. He looked both frightened and intrigued. It was funny to see him try to hide his expression.

"Come on, Chandler, I'll show you around."

She got up to follow me through the house. I had other things in mind. We stopped in the kitchen to refresh our drinks. As I mixed, I asked questions.

"So, how long have you two been dating?"

"I wouldn't really call it dating. We've been out a few times."

"He seems like a nice guy."

"He's been a total gentleman."

"That's great. Well, follow me."

I walked her through the house, showing her room after room. We got to my little sanctuary.

"This was the selling point," I said as I opened the door.

"Nice."

"Step in, let me show you," I said as I let her pass me.

"This is a great book collection," she said as she walked over to the bookcase.

I stepped in and closed the door. "This is the best part of it all," I said as I locked it. "So no one can bother you."

"Yes, but listen: I can't hear a thing going on outside that door--It's sound proof."

"Tell me a little about yourself, Chandler. We don't get to talk much."

"Nothing much to tell. I live life."

She sat on my bench next to the bookcase. She looked at me squarely. I wasn't fooling her and I could tell. I found my place seated next to her.

"Tell me what you really want. I know you and all the other 'ladies' at church don't think highly of me. They don't try to hide it."

"On the contrary, I have no reserved judgement. I actually admire your carefreeness."

"It didn't seem that way when I walked in here."

"I was just shocked to see you is all. I wasn't aware you and Marvin were dating."

"Like I said, I wouldn't call it dating."

"Well, he's a good catch; promising career, goal oriented, church going..."

"It would be nice but, I don't think he's interested."

"Why wouldn't he be? You're a very attractive woman."

"Thank you. That means a lot coming from you."

"What do you mean coming from me?"

"Let's be real, Ms. Maxine, you're smoking hot. Forgive me if that sounds inappropriate."

"Not at all, Chandler," I began. "I'm flattered you think so." I reached over and gently eased her hair behind her ear with my forefinger and told her, "You are quite attractive. I can't see why Marvin wouldn't want you."

I only did it at first to see how she would react. She didn't seem surprised at all, nor did she flinch, which made me want to see how far she would actually let me go. She blushed a bit. But, I backed off. I got up, walked to the bookshelf.

"You like to read?"

"I read some."

"What type of books do you like? Maybe I have something you can borrow."

"I doubt you read the type of books I do."

"You'd be surprised, Chandler. Just because I'm a lady of the church doesn't mean I'm not a lady all the same."

"Still, I doubt it."

"Let me read you something. You tell me if you like it."

"Ok," she said as she sipped some more of her drink.

I fingered the books, looking for just the right one. "Here's something. Now, tell me if it's too much for you."

"I doubt it," she said with a chuckle.

I began reading,

"Oh, don't look at me with that 'I'm so innocent' face, Tanya said, looking at Destiny as she sipped from her glass.

"But, I am innocent, Destiny said as she sat her glass on the cocktail table in front of them.

"My eye.

"Destiny leaned over to Tanya and kissed her lips ever-so-slightly, then said, I can't help that sometimes I just have to express how I'm feeling.

"Sometimes? You always feel sexy.

"That is so not true, Destiny said into Tanya's ear as she caressed her leg.

"Tanya allowed her head to fall back on the couch as she closed her eyes. *See that's what I mean*, she thought but she dared not say a word because she didn't want her to stop.

"Destiny continued to speak. Is there anything wrong with feeling sexy?

"Tanya just shook her head as Destiny's hands roamed her legs and found their way between her thighs.

"You wore this dress on purpose, didn't you?

"Tanya didn't respond. Destiny's fingers parted those lower lips as she continued to whisper into Tanya's ear.

"Oh, so now you can't hear me? You wore this dress just for this purpose, didn't you? Destiny asked as her fingers entered Tanya's warm chasm.

"Ahhhhhh, Tanya moaned in pleasure.

"Answer me. You wore this dress on purpose, didn't you?

"Umm-hmm, she moaned in response."

While reading I'd slowly made my way over to Chandler, and as I stood in front of her, I looked down and made eye-contact.

"Is that the type of book you like to read?"

She was fanning as I looked down at her. I almost felt sorry for her. She had no idea she was a pawn in my game.

"I love that type of book, Ms. Maxine," she said as she looked up at me.

When her eyes met mine, she turned away. I again swept her hair behind her ear and gently guided her face so that our eyes met yet again.

"Don't be afraid to show me who you really are. Your secrets are safe in here. This room is sound proof, remember?"

She smiled at me and chuckled a bit.

"Shall I keep reading?"

"Please do. I'm excited to hear what happens next."

"So am I--excited that is."

I continued,

"See you just…Tanya attempted to say something between breaths.

"What? I can't hear you, Destiny said, now pulled back so she could get a full view of Tanya's face.

"You…you…just…have to…play.

"But, you like how I play, don't you? This is what you wanted, right?

"Mmmm, Yeeeeeeesss!

"I thought so. Give me what I'm looking for, Destiny demanded.

"She continued to probe her digits deeper. Tanya bucked against her appendages as if her life depended on it.

"Ahhhh…I'm…I'm cumming! Tanya exclaimed.

"Yeah, that's just what I want."

I closed the book. "I better stop there, it's getting a little warm in here."

"Well, I want to know what happens."

"Curious, are you?"

"Yes, yes I am."

She was fully aware of what I was asking with my double-sided question. I knew it and she knew I knew as she looked directly in my face with her answer.

"Here, take it with you. Start from the beginning. Bring it back whenever you like," I said as I handed her the book

"I like hearing it come from your lips," she said with a dejected look.

"You like watching my lips?"

She didn't respond.

I leaned down to get closer as if I thought she couldn't hear me. I spoke so closely to her ear that I knew she could feel my breath on her skin.

"Do you like my lips, Chandler?"

She turned and kissed me, softly and gingerly.

"I do in fact."

I pulled away, stood erect.

"I'm sure you wore this nice dress for Marvin but I quite enjoyed watching you walk in it. Stand for me. Turn around."

She stood and did a little turn as I stepped back.

"I like the way it fits you. Turn a little more slowly for me; I might want to get one for myself."

She continued turning. I placed my hands on her hips and held her steady so that she stopped with her back to me.

"Wait there. I want to see how short it is. My husband gets a little nervous if my skirts are too short."

"It's not really short at all."

"You fill it in well though. He has a
problem when I have to pick things up. Bend over
for me, let me see if it shows too much."

"I'm not sure if I should."

"Why? There's no one here but us. They
won't see."

She bent over and I could see what I already
knew. She wasn't wearing underwear. Her mound
looked plump and moist and I imagined it tasted
like a fluffy cupcake. I bit my nail to try to control
the next action that came to mind.

"Can you see under there, Ms. Maxine?"

"Not too much at that angle. What if you
were placing something in the bottom of a grocery
basket?"

She bent down some more and I just
couldn't help myself. Before I knew it, my face
was buried in her ass. She'd leaned her head and
one knee on that bench in front of her, opening up
her glory for me to get every bit of it. It had been a
long time since I'd tasted some sweet nectar that
wasn't my own. I lapped and twisted my tongue
just as Marvin had done before in this very room.
Her moans made me keep going and I wanted to see
how far she would go. My fingers found their way

into her sweet, wet pussy and she took every one I had to offer. I rubbed a finger across her anus to see if she'd take that, too. I had to save something for next time, though. There was still something missing, and I had plans for her swirling in my head. All the things I thought of nearly brought me to a climax, but she had to go first. My fingers wiggled and penetrated as far as they could go. When she released, her moans were so erotic that they gave me a climax of my own.

When I was finished, she looked as if she should be ashamed.

"Honey, there's more where that came from. You keep my secret; I'll keep yours."

"Ms. Maxine, I would never tell a soul."

"Good, I can take you places you've never been. And I'll help you get that man out there to give you the kind of attention that you want."

We left the room and joined the others as if nothing happened.

The Web

About a month had passed before I got Chandler back over. Not because she didn't want to come, but because of scheduling conflicts and other sorts of things. There was plenty priming I'd completed, though. We'd been texting and I had a full understanding of how far I could take her. In the meantime, I'd been feeding her tidbits of things to draw Marvin in. He of course, had no clue I was coaching her or even that I was aware of their half-baked relationship.

I'd seen them at church of course, and each time I saw them together I did something to gain reassurance that I still had Marvin on my hook. Hence, the little rendezvous in the shower. I was fine with him filling his downtime with a play thing as long as I knew I still had my place as a priority thing. I'd even help her keep him as long as I had control over either of them. They had no idea the depth of the game I played, or what the stakes were.

Chandler liked to play coy but I knew she wasn't. I was the master at that game and there was no way she could beat me at it. I did like her though. She reminded me of myself when I was her age. Keeping her on my hook was a must. The possibilities I saw with her were endless, and coupled with Marvin, I'd be satisfied until the end of time.

It was cool out and I'd invited Chandler over to have drinks outside by the pool with me. She'd been trying to return my book, and this was the perfect day to do so. The kids were away for the weekend, and Jason was facilitating a singles' workshop at the church. I had most of the day and late into the evening to do with her as I pleased.

There was a knock at the door.

"Come on in. I'm in the kitchen," I yelled.

I was standing at the counter in my little sundress I liked to lounge around in, preparing a fruit tray.

"Ms. Maxine?"

"I'm right here," I said as she rounded the corner into my kitchen.

She looked fresh, bright and refreshed.

"I brought the juice you asked for."

"Just sit it right there. I was getting us some fruit to nibble on. Come on out here. Bring the juice."

I picked up the tray and walked out onto the patio to sit the tray on the table. She sat the juice on the table.

"Have a seat, darling," I said as I took the juice to open it.

There was a glass pitcher sitting on the table filled with champagne, just waiting for its companion.

"Nothing like mimosas in the morning." Chandler said as she lifted her glass.

We sat there, ate fruit, drank and chit-chatted a bit as if we didn't have other business on the floor. Sitting there watching her mouth move made me want to see just how skilled she was.

"I see you brought the book back. Did you enjoy it?"

127

"Yeah, it was intense to say the least. That Destiny was something else."

"Yes, she was."

"I have others I'm sure you'll like. Come on, let's go find you one."

She stood up and started toward the back where my private room was. We stopped in the kitchen to refill the mimosa pitcher. I followed behind, watching her hips sway with the flow of the maxi-dress I'm sure she wore in anticipation of what really was going on here.

As we stepped through the door, I pulled it closed to make her feel more secure. We were in my sanctuary and nothing could penetrate it. She walked over to the bookcase and replaced the book, "Recipe of Deception" she'd borrowed.

"I see you have more books here by the same author. I'd like to read those."

"Go ahead, honey, just make sure I get those back. They're signed."

"I noticed that, that's why I wanted to make sure I got it back to you."

"Let me fill your glass," I said as I topped off her flute.

"If I didn't know any better I'd swear you were trying to get me drunk."

"No need for that. Were you drunk the last time we were here?"

"I was a little tipsy."

"Well, let's go for tipsy so I can see what other things I can get you to do."

She blushed, but that's not the girl I wanted to see today. I wanted that girl she kept trying to hide.

"Ms. Maxine, you are a trip."

"I'm more than that! I would tell you to stop putting Ms. In front of my name, but I kinda like it."

"Would you prefer mistress?"

"You're not ready for that, honey."

"So, you say."

"Show me different then, honey."

"Show me what else you have hidden in here. I've heard your husband boast about how you spend hours in your own sanctuary. I know you do more than reading."

129

She lifted the seat on my bench.

"I don't know if you can handle what's in there. They say curiosity killed the cat."

"I'm looking to get my cat killed."

That's the girl I wanted to see!

She started digging around in my toy chest. I sat across on the chaise sipping my drink, observing her reaction the more she dug. She didn't say much, paused every now and again to take a drink, pulled things out, then put them back. I paid special attention to the things she paid extra attention to.

"Chandler, let me ask you something. What do you really want from me?"

"I want to…" When she turned to look at me, she saw all my glory. I'd sat with my legs agape. My short, house dress fell to my waist. Her words caught in her throat.

"What's the matter?"

"Nothing, Ms. Maxine."

"Let me ask you a question, Chandler. I want us to be open with each other. I'm not trying

130

to get too personal but I want to be personal. Has
Marvin tasted that sweet pussy yet?"

"No," she said with a little sadness in her
voice.

"Well, if he knew what I knew, he wouldn't
wait another minute."

"I'm curious about something, Ms. Maxine,
and forgive me if I'm too forward."

"If you haven't figured out that there's no
such thing with me yet, I don't know what to tell
you. What's on your mind, darling?"

"I want to know what you taste like."

"Honey, come get it. I thought you'd never ask. I
want to know what those lips feel like."

She walked over, got on her knees and
leaned into my pussy so she could lap up my juices.
Her lips felt as soft as cotton as they touched my
sweet spot. When her tongue parted my lips I felt
the warmth. She played with it; at first barely
grazing my clit, curling her tongue as if she was
trying to ease me into it. When she took me fully in
her mouth, I gasped. Oh, Chandler stopped playing
with me and showed me she knew exactly what she
was doing and what she wanted. She started talking
to me between suction.

131

"I've been wanting to do this for so long."

"Oooo, baby, I wish you had," I moaned as I caressed her hair.

I started grinding into her face as if her tongue was a dick. As I held her head there I started talking to her. "This is what you wanted-- what you've been waiting for."

She could do nothing but move her head. I wouldn't allow her to pull her lips from my center. My head fell back but my hips didn't stop. I thought I heard something so I lifted my head. There stood Marvin in the door, watching. The smirk that crossed my lips was all-telling. Chandler didn't know he was there. She was enjoying her treat, but I kept talking. "Yes, baby, get that pussy. Make me cum!"

She sucked harder, played more, inserted two fingers into my wanting pussy. I was grinding even harder.

"I want to see you take a dick while you do that. Can I?"

Again she nodded, not wanting to take her lips from that honey pot. Marvin stood there stroking his dick. I'd sat up a bit, reaching further down to pull Chandler's dress up, exposing her

plump, round ass. I rubbed it and slapped it as I
looked into Marvin's eyes.

"Chandler, would you do it for me?" I
pulled her hair away so she could answer.

"I'd do anything for you, Ms. Maxine."

I forced her face back in my pussy and she
continued to please me. I continued to grind on her
tongue. Marvin had moved closer, quietly taking
his clothes off along the way. Chandler was no
fool. She knew something was up by now, but she
played along. She'd paused once, but then dived
back in with more veracity. I leaned forward again,
rubbing and gripping her meaty ass. This time, I
spread it open for him to see, inviting him in. He
stood behind her, erect and ready. Marvin knelt at
her back and I looked into his eyes as he slid his
sheathed sword into her wetness. I could tell from
the look on his face she felt good. I felt a tinge of
jealousy come over me. Chandler stopped what she
was doing to catch her breath.

I pulled her hair and stuffed her face deeper
in my pussy before I said, "Don't stop, take that
dick and lick this pussy. Make me feel what you
feeling from that dick." I watched her get pounded
as I looked into Marvin's eyes. All the while, I felt
her tongue. This wasn't all I had in store for her.

I slid from under her, bent over and whispered in her ear. I looked up at Marvin. "Don't stop, honey, she's been waiting on that. Give it to her," I said as I walked over to my toy chest.

I dug around until I found what I was looking for. After closing the bench, I sat there and watched them. Her ass rippled as he pumped into her. I walked over to Marvin and kissed him. He accepted my tongue and with it he knew my thoughts. When I pulled away from him, he pulled out of her.

Chandler turned around wondering why he'd stopped. She saw us standing side by side. She didn't cower, instead she licked her lips. He stood at full attention and my purchased "attention" matched his. She looked back and forth at the both of us.

"Ms. Maxine, what do you want me to do?"

She spoke to me but looked at him.

"You two switch places. I want to see you suck his dick."

She did just as I asked and made sure to prop her ass in the air just for me. I couldn't resist tasting her sweetness. The way her ass sat wide open made me want to see what it felt like with my tongue. I went back and forth wetting them both with my saliva.

"Get up there and ride that dick," I told her.

I watched her mount him and slide down so gingerly. She rocked as if she were adjusting to him. Chandler moved as he filled every inch of her. I knew the motion well.

"Don't get timid on me. Do what you have been wanting to do," I said as I grabbed her hips and made the motion for her to bounce.

I got behind her and straddled Marvin's legs, I was close enough for her to feel the rubber dick on her ass and matched her motions. I caressed her breasts from behind and began kissing her neck and shoulders. Her head fell back and eyes closed as she enjoyed every motion and touch. After peering over her shoulder, looking into Marvin's eyes, I wanted to punish her for pleasing him.

Her head was now pushed to his chest with my hand on the back of her neck. I'd caused her to slow her motion and demanded she stay still. I took my rubber dick and guided it into her ass. She tried to run but neither of us would let her. Marvin held her hips in place while I held her neck with one hand. I entered her slowly, applying just enough pressure to press my dick deeper. She took a deep breath as the full length of my plastic penis entered her anus.

"Ms. Maxine?"

"Yes, honey," I responded.

She began to rock on Marvin's dick as she laid fully to his chest.

"Fuck me, Ms. Maxine. Take all that you want."

"Oh yes! Honey."

I did just that. I watched my dick go in and out of her ass as Marvin's dick went in and out of her pussy below me. I wanted to cum but I needed to hold on. Pants, moans, and grunts filled the room. That room had been transformed into a state of euphoria which we were all wrapped up in. I heard Marvin's grunts get deeper and I knew he was ready to let go. I pumped faster and Marvin pumped hard. Before I knew it, I had a hand full of Chandler's hair.

"Look at him when you cum and tell him who you belong to."

She moaned and panted.

"Tell him!"

"Who do you belong to?" he asked.

"Ms. Maxine," she screamed as we all climaxed together.

It took me a minute to catch my breath as I slid my dick from her ass. She rolled off of Marvin and sat on the floor.

"That was entertaining," we heard a voice from the door say.

I turned around and saw Jason standing there.

"How long have you been there?" I asked him.

"Long enough."

"Marvin, I thought you closed the door."

"It was closed, dear, but it wasn't locked," Jason said.

"Pastor, I can explain," Chandler tried to interject.

"There is nothing to explain, dear," he interrupted.

Marvin just laid there without a word.

"But, Pastor, I'm sorry, I…"

He cut her off again.

"There's nothing to be sorry for."

I tried to calm her. "Chandler, it's ok."

She stood, pulling down her dress that had been gathered around her waist.

"I don't know how to make this up to you."

As soon as she said that I knew she'd opened a door she wasn't going to be ready to walk through.

"Well, come here, child," Jason said to her.

All the while, I'd removed my plastic appendage and wrapped it in a towel to clean later. My dress, which was also around my waist, was now down, fully covering me. I'd poured myself another drink as I took this all in. Marvin had pulled on his clothes. As Jason now stood in the middle of the floor, Chandler walked over to him. He put his hands on her shoulders.

"You want to make it up to me?" he asked her.

"Yes, sir."

"Then, get this nut out my dick," he demanded as he pushed her to her knees.

She looked confused as she got on her knees and looked to me for approval.

"Don't look at her. She follows my orders. Nothing goes on in this house I haven't already orchestrated. You're not hers, you're mine now."

Chandler looked shocked and hurt, but there was still a twinge of fire in her eyes.

"You do like being punished, don't you?" I said as I realized she wanted it.

"I think I need some alone time with this one," Jason said.

Marvin and I both started towards the door.

"Oh yes, I'm going to have fun with this one," Jason said just before I heard the door lock as we exited.

"You aren't going to be her buffer?" Marvin asked.

"I told her curiosity killed the cat. He can have her so, I can have you."   END

A Detroit native, Kaylynn grew up on the east side of the city and has always had an insatiable passion for writing. She graduated from Detroit Public Schools. Kaylynn began her family early; she was married at the age of 23. She went on to pursue a career as a licensed electrician while balancing a household and three children. She found herself divorced by the age of 28. The economic climate of the city came crashing to a halt forcing her to look at other venues. Kaylynn realized that being a work horse was not what fulfilled her. She chose to show her three sons that it's never too late to follow your dreams. Kaylynn lives in a suburban area of Metropolitan Detroit.

She enjoys reading and spending time with her family and many friends. Kaylynn is not easily influenced by the 'norm' and it comes across on her pages. She challenges the conventional.

Successful, confident, creative, attractive and

independent are some of many ways to describe this Detroit business woman. Savannah never would've been considered a one man woman. Variety had always been the spice of her life and she wasn't sure she would be satisfied in any other way. When the man of her dreams crash lands in her life, she begins to rethink the path she followed. Just when she was attempting to throw in her hand of player's cards, chaos ensues. For once in her life Savannah finds herself in a situation her slick talk and carefree attitude won't get her out of. Consequences soon catch up with her and it is a matter of life or the forever after.

Lucas and Moreen Harrison appear to be a happy  couple on the surface. But they say never judge a book by its cover. This one is no different. Lucas is a man who only wants to take care of his family and thrive in business. But he finds the haunts of a past love and life too distracting. He becomes mesmerized by a gorgeous woman with a beautiful soul, unaware of her good and bad intentions.

Moreen craves intimacy that has been lacking on the home front. She allows herself to be charmed and swept off her feet by a Casanova found in an unlikely place. Confident that her husband would just about allow anything rather than be alone, she finds power to immerse herself in this sea of seduction.

The two are caught in a web of lies they unknowingly weaved together. This ordinary love triangle takes another shape all of its own. Both thought their truths would be hidden from the light.

Neither of them realizes they are in the hands of Destiny.

www.KaylynnHunt.com
www.Kaylynn@KaylynnHunt.com

Follow her on Instagram @: Kaylynnhunt

Only For One Night

Chapter One

"Nothing here but old farts and young junk," her colleague snarled, looking around the back-alley dive in disappointment.

Morgan's feet hurt, and she wasn't about to go back outside in thirty-degree weather until she was positive the cab was right outside the door.

"I'm getting a drink," Morgan said. "Sit your butt down until the guy calls. You told him thirty minutes, right?"

Slumping in the booth across from Morgan, Vicki Turner huffed. "I can't believe the one night you want some, you can't find any. I bet your nasty cousin is out there fucking the whole Chicago and you're going back home dry as a bone."

Morgan shrugged, massaging her feet. "It was a foolhardy idea. Terra has always been able to find the good ones."

"Could you put your shoes on?" Vicki scoffed, disgusted. But, Morgan knew her friend just wanted something to complain about.

Wearing three-inch heels and trying to walk from bar to bar had been a bad idea, but Morgan thought she had gotten dressed up for something. For a thick girl like herself, having the confidence to go out and show what her Momma gave her took a lot of work.

They were out of town on business and it was her first free night in a couple of months, so she decided to take a chance. She wanted to find a no-strings-attached kind of guy she could bring back to the hotel room her company was paying for, and just enjoy herself. The last six bars they'd found were full of sad, pathetic men.

Chicago sucked!

The door to the dive opened, whipping cold air though the place and the biggest, hottest looking man this side of the Mississippi filled the doorway.

"Damn! Look what answered our prayers," Vicki sang.

Morgan kicked her with her bare foot.

"Eww!" Vicki said. "Don't put those stinky dogs on me."

Morgan giggled, knowing fully well her feet didn't stink, but her giggle caught his attention. His dark almond eyes looked directly at her as if she had been what he had been looking for all night long, and his eyes went down to her feet. One of her shoes was still off, and he looked at her toes like he wanted to thread his thick tongue between them, despite everyone watching.

All of a sudden, Morgan felt uncomfortable and put her shoes back on. Looking away she said, "He is kinda on the big side, don't you think, Vick? Big is not my forte."

Vicki licked her lips voraciously. "That boy's been extra-dipped in a big bowl of Hershey's chocolate. You better jump on him before I do."

Morgan was glad the waitress came over and asked them for their drink order. The distraction from trying to look over at the big guy, who was now at the bar talking with the bartender, disturbed her.

"We'll take two very strong Manhattans!" Vicki declared.

As thirsty as Morgan was, she wasn't trying to get drunk, but she didn't stop the order.

"Your phone charged, right?" she asked, wondering how long thirty minutes were.

"Gurl, this is your chance to relieve some stress. Give that guy the eye so he can get over here and take you home," Vicki snarled.

Morgan was suddenly shy. That man had looked at her like she was the air he needed to breathe, and she wasn't into some guy fostering an addiction to her. It took forever to get rid of Kevin.

"That man's a tall drink of water," Vicki began. "And with us going back to Detroit tomorrow, you need to get your thirst quenched tonight!"

The man tucked something into his jacket from the bartender, picked up the Jameson on the Rocks he'd ordered, and tossed it back into his mouth. He said something to the bartender and then looked directly at Morgan.

Damn, I wish I was his drink!

The waitress came back over and placed the Manhattans in front of them. "The handsome guy at the bar is paying for your drinks. He said compliments of the lady in blue and that it's his favorite color."

Morgan looked over at Vicki and realized the waitress was talking about the simple, royal blue dress she'd borrowed from her cousin, Terra.

Blushing from root to tip, she realized she hadn't had a one night stand since college, and now at thirty-four years old, she was feeling like a virgin, even though she wasn't.

Vicki's phone buzzed. "And that's my cue," she said standing up. "You have a good night."

"Wait, Vicki," Morgan said jumping up, following her to the door. "I don't know him!"

"That's the point!" Vicki said and rushed out of the door.

Morgan was about to follow, but realized she hadn't put her shoes on and it was cold as hell outside.

Turning back around to the bar, the large stranger had moved over to her booth and picked up her shoes. He dangled them from his pinky finger, and even that looked large.

147

As she walked up to him, she swore the man lifted steel containers for fun and she so wished she had not stopped smoking ten years ago.

He extended the other large hand at her. "My friends call me Luke." His voice was thick and he seized her with crotch-quivering eye-contact.

She was glad her Manhattan was still on the table.

Morgan raised her eyes up past his wide chest, thick arms, broad shoulders and thick neck to a godly-chiseled, dark-skinned face and a tight goatee. His hair was dark and not a strand seemed to be out of place.

Licking her lips, she said, "My friends call me May." She started to take a deeper look at him.

In his dark, expensive Italian suit, Bulgari watch, freshly groomed nails and handmade Italian shoes, (for his exceptionally large feet) he was too handsome for words and suddenly she knew he was out of his element.

"You don't come here often, do you?" she asked skeptically.

He blushed. "I told your friend if you're a smart woman you'd figure that out."

Confused, Morgan raised a brow. "You know my friend?"

"Yes, she approached me in the lobby this morning at your hotel while you were busy making some arrangements. I was speaking to the bartender there. Asked if I was in town alone and would I like some company tonight. I wasn't interested in her, but then she showed me a picture of you."

Worriedly, she asked, "It wasn't the…oh, lawd, please say she didn't!"

"Orange suits you very well."

Morgan wanted to die from embarrassment. Two years ago, she was dragged on a trip to California, and Vicki got her in a too-tight bikini, snapping a picture right before she nearly burst from the garment.

"I told her to delete that photo!" she hissed.

He smiled gratefully. "I'm glad your friend didn't. I was speechless and impressed." His eyes drifted down her body and then back up again in a visual caress that made her heart race.

"I can't believe Vicki set me up."

He pointed to the booth, and she sat down. When he knelt down in front of her and took a foot to put on her shoes, she wanted to die again from the embarrassment. Morgan felt as if someone touching her feet was too intimate.

"Oddly, she said that's what *you* do," he noted. "She explained you're always doing for everyone else and you never have time for yourself."

Rolling her eyes around, Morgan said, "I never imagined I had a nose for helping others until I found my daughter a perfect man."

He stopped what he was doing and just held her toes tightly. His hands were so damn warm. "You married your daughter off, May?"

"Well, yes, she's twenty-one. They're getting married in a month."

Frowning, he questioned, "You have a twenty-one year-old daughter?"

Blushing, she said, "I wasn't always the good girl. I was rather promiscuous in my olden days."

"How old are you?"

"My birthday was two days ago. I turned thirty-four. I was birthing my daughter and graduating from high school at the same time. Luckily, my mother made me go to community college at night and work during the day for two straight years to get my life together so I could raise my daughter and get a decent job to support myself."

"Wow, beauty, brains and a hard worker. Rare in a woman these days." He finished strapping on her other shoe, but didn't move from his kneeling position and didn't take her foot off his thigh. His hand casually rested on her ankle. "So, why is an extraordinary woman like you having such difficulties in finding a good man?"

Leaning in close, she said, "Because, sometimes it's not always a good man people are looking for, Luke. It's the right man."

He smirked. "I didn't think I would enjoy meeting you, but I must ask; would you grant me the pleasure of your company tonight, May?"

"Was that difficult to formulate?"

He chuckled. "With your name, I'd sound like a complete idiot saying, 'May, may I have?'"

She laughed with him.

Damn! She hadn't laughed with a man in a very long while. Licking her lips again, she said, "I would be honored for you to join me in my room tonight, Luke."

Suddenly, he looked uncomfortable and put her foot down. "I have a better idea. I know your friend will be waiting for you to come back to the hotel tonight with me. Let's keep her guessing and find another hotel, my treat?" He held out his large, strong hand for her to take. Briefly, she noted that there was a ring missing from his left hand, but she hoped in the back of her mind that that meant he was recently divorced.

Morgan didn't know what she was getting herself into, but this man was so damn handsome she didn't want to care. "Lead the way," she insisted, taking his hand, guiding him out of the dive.

Chapter Two

There was a black sedan outside waiting for them with a driver who ushered them in from the cold into the back seat.

"You arranged all this with Vicki?" she asked skeptically.

"I was coming to this bar anyway tonight, and I asked your friend to meet me here around the time you arrived. You were a little late, but I didn't mind waiting."

She noted he seemed very interested in talking with bartenders around Chicago, but made no mention of that observation. One of her superpowers was picking up on the things people chose not to say. It was a blessing and curse.

Tonight, she needed a blessing; a very orgasmic blessing, and if Vicki had checked him out already, Morgan was determined to enjoy herself.

"So, what did Vicki tell you about me?" she inquired.

"She said you were very hard working, loved your family and friends, sacrificed for people you cared about and did everything in your power to make everyone else happy except yourself. She asked me to make you happy…for one night." He leaned in close to her. "When was the last time your lips were thoroughly kissed, May?"

Sadly, she couldn't remember. "I recollected when I was on a date a couple of years ago, but it was so sloppy, I don't want to try to remember. The experience dissuaded me to stop dating."

"That bad?" he asked.

"It was horrible. There was a river above my lip I had to swipe a couple of times to clean off."

"I think I can help repair that memory," he said.

"You think?"

He chuckled sensuously. "You'll have to close your eyes."

Morgan breathlessly shuddered as she closed her eyes. He moved even closer to her, and his breath brushed the top of her lip. She could smell the Irish whiskey just before his warm lips pressed against hers in the perfect slant. He pressed up slightly, drawing the breath out of her, making her forget to take more in as he pressed again in a deeper slant. This time not so perfect, but making her gasp and then moan. Slowly, he straightened up, rubbed her nose to his and moved away.

"Did that help you forget?" he asked.

"Forget what?"

Again, he chuckled sensuously. "You have a delightful sense of humor."

In all honesty, she had forgotten what he had been trying to make her forget. She just wanted to find a way to get kissed again. "Do I get a reward for that?"

Luke didn't need to ask what kind of reward she was expecting from him. This time, his arms came around her waist, and he seemed to slide her across the seat until her side was molded against his. His lips returned to hers.

This time, she was ready to show him some of her passionate kissing skills, and before long, he seemed lost in her lips. Luke's tongue delved into her mouth and entwined with hers as if he were meant to be there and they had been kissing for centuries.

A voice cleared several times, and they realized the car had stopped in front of another hotel. He reluctantly slid her to her side of the vehicle and nodded to the driver.

When they were in the lobby, she let him go to the desk to make arrangements for a room. He joined her almost too quickly and led her to an elevator.

When he pushed the top button and used his key to trigger the elevator, she looked at him curiously.

"How did you reserve the penthouse?" she questioned.

"I have some friends around town. They keep a room here for clients." He winked and pulled her into his embrace. "Now, where were we?"

His large body had to stoop down to kiss her, but she didn't mind at all. Going up to a penthouse, kissing a very handsome man was what most women dreamed of.

His hands immediately cupped her full-figured rear and kneaded her hips. One hand came around and fondled her breasts. She, in turn, touched his wide chest, moved down his rippled stomach and moved over his hardened shaft that seemed to want to burst out of his pants.

Morgan determined he would be a nice lover although the feel of his girth had her worried.

She was barely cognizant of getting off the elevator and making their way to a door. He couldn't stop kissing her, and when they were inside of the penthouse, he may have flickered one light.

There was just enough light to make their way to a bedroom. Between kissing, desperate touching and the rubbing of their bodies together, they knew one thing; they wanted each other.

She turned around so he could undo her dress. It was as if he read her mind, quickly pulling the zipper down, kissing her neck, unhooking her bra, and helping her out of her garment. When she turned to him, her black bra fell from her body. He gasped in amazement.

"Damn!" He whispered so low if there had been any other noise like music playing, she didn't think she would have heard him. He dropped to his knees in front of her. Her five-foot-two height, even on her heels was still a challenge to him, but he curved her body so his mouth could suckle her large dark nipples.

His large hands were perfect for her forty-D cup breasts, and his worship of them almost made her cry.

He stood up, abruptly lifting her with him by her ass. His mouth returned to hers as he carried her over to the bed and then laid her on her back, sideways away from the pillows.

She whimpered as he left the bed to strip out of his clothes. When he returned to her, he pulled down her panties. She was about to take off her shoes, but he stopped her.

"Leave them on for later," he ordered.

She heard a condom package tear and she fully relaxed, glad he was taking precautions.

Luke was fully hardened as he pressed into her. The dim light from the other room outlined his large, muscular body and she was very right about his girth. Despite her being very wet, Luke's thickness still challenged her.

Worriedly, he asked, "Do you need some lubrication?"

Just the way he said those words made her think of him providing natural lubrication for her down there with those sexy lips of his. A flood of her essence leaked all over, giving him enough natural lubrication where he pushed right in.

They both gasped, amazed that she had taken in so much of him. With a deliciously snug fit, Luke was learning her body, mastering the spots that seemed to excite her most. His reward; more natural lubrication so he could ease even more of himself into her.

She became so aroused she could feel a river running between the crack of her rear as he pushed more and more into her. Soon, he was to the hilt and then ground deeply within her.

Moaning and scratching his back, bucking up into his body, passionately kissing him, loving every centimeter of his largeness over her and inside of her; he thickened more.

"Ugh...my...Gawd!" she cried as each stroke took her to an out-of-this-world plateau.

And he joined her, growling right before he buried his face in her neck.

She giggled, loving how he carefully didn't put all his weight on her. "That was fun."

Chapter Three

After a few minutes, he raised up from her and though he was limp, she could feel a substantial pull out. It took a moment for her body to adjust from his circumference and she closed her eyes and smiled, trying to remember everything she was feeling.

He'd walked out of the room, but returned shortly. "Damn, woman, you look like you want some more," he said, taking her hands and guiding her to stand up.

Morgan admitted, "I haven't had sex in a very long time."

"How long?" he inquired.

"Four years to be exact." She pushed the sadness away. "After my mother died, my fiancé-to-be decided he couldn't cope with my depression and decided to step away. I haven't seen him since the funeral."

"Damn! That is cold blooded." He continued to guide her around the hotel room to the bathroom. The shower was going and he pulled her inside using his body to shield her from the water. "You sure it wasn't for something else? I'm shocked a beautiful woman like you haven't been touched by a man in so very long." He was soaping up a washcloth and started to wash her up.

This was a unique gesture for Morgan because no man had bathed her. This fine nucca was not only cleaning every nook and cranny on her body, but he was also arousing her at the same time.

She had to think for a moment before responding to his question. "I'm a workaholic, which doesn't help me find anyone. I guess my friend felt bad for me, knowing how long I've been celibate."

He looked impressed as he kissed her collarbone and then moved down to her breasts with the washcloth. "You must love your job."

"I do…I mean, I did, until I came here."

By this time, he was moving down to her stomach and lowering his body so his face was down there, too. The shower water rinsed away the soap on her chest and streamed down her body.

"What happened?"

"Our company is being bought out by this other company, and we came here to strike a deal with the new owners. The guy that's buying us out didn't have the balls to show up. It's like he wants to throw his money around and just expect us to accept everything. He doesn't understand how hard we worked for this company to be successful, and in my opinion, he doesn't care."

He paused for a moment as he circled the cloth around her stomach, moving his arms around her waist to look up at her. "He could've been busy doing something stupid or important. Life always gets in the way of things."

"Are you defending him?" she asked incredulously.

"I'm just a sympathetic businessman who understands life," he explained.

"He should have been busy taking care of business and had his butt at that meeting."

He started kissing on her stomach and then used the tip of his tongue to tickle her belly button.

His hands were soaping up her thighs and rear, while his mouth moved down between her legs.

"Wait," she whispered, but forgot what she was going to say as she felt his chin circle her clitoris. His fingers parted her lower lips, and she could feel the water drizzle down between her legs. A finger pressed into her as he used his chin to increase the stimulation on her most sensitive part. His mouth licked the corners near her thighs and planted kissed in her bed of hair.

It was just too erotic for Morgan, and she was once again propelled into the sensuous unknown, enjoying her orgasm to the fullest. It was a good thing he was down there holding her steady because her legs buckled more than once, unable to hold up her weight.

When her senses had come back to reality, he was finishing up by her feet, washing each toe as if he had an agenda for them later.

He stood back up and moved his big body to the side to let her rinse off. Kissing the breath from her, he gently slapped her ass and said, "Order us something to snack on while I finish up in here. Charge it to the room."

She stepped out of the shower and grabbed a guest towel.

After ordering a fruit tray, she grabbed her phone and saw that Vicki had texted her several times.

Morgan saw her friend's worry and texted back, "I'm fine. He's fine, and we're at a hotel together. I'll see you when I get back later."

Putting her phone down, she made sure her clothes were gathered in a chair by the door. By that time the shower stopped and someone knocked on the hotel's door.

He called out from the bathroom, "Get in bed. I'll take care of them."

Doing as he ordered, she watched as he came from the bedroom with a guest robe that barely closed around his large body. He grabbed a money clip out of his pants and went to the hotel door.

When he returned to the bedroom, he was carrying the tray of food she had ordered. With just her towel around her body, she didn't feel like she had any clothes on.

"Are you hungry yet?" he questioned.

Slowly, she shook her head and looked down at his robe. His member was still limp, and she understood he needed time to "refresh" himself.

164

He put the tray on the table and moved to the end of the bed. "Are your feet still sore?"

She only shrugged.

Gently picking up her foot, his strong fingers began to massage her heel. Their eyes met, and she blushed. He was clearly enjoying giving her a foot rub as much as she enjoyed receiving the foot rub.

His mouth dipped down and kissed the center of her foot, and then he planted small kisses up to her toes where he also kissed each tip. He looked at her again. By this time she had bitten down on her lip and was waiting breathlessly for what he was going to do next.

He dragged his lips across the bottom of her toes and planted wet kisses all down her feet to her heels.

The sensation was ticklish and erotic at the same time.

Morgan was not surprised when he picked up her other foot and did the same thing, but this time, he took his time on each toe, sucking, licking and laving around, all the while massaging her foot, then her calves and then moving up to her thighs.

She was in blissful arousal by then as he crawled up her body with kisses, moving her towel aside.

Pushing his robe off his broad shoulders, she lifted her body up and kissed him recklessly. His hardened manhood laid above her womanhood. He was ready for her and they rolled around on the bed until she straddled his waist. He quickly put his hand in the robe's pocket and produced another condom. She took this one from him, scooted down while opening the package, but didn't put the condom on immediately.

Morgan wanted to return the favor and orally excite the various parts of him between his legs. She kissed his thighs and then moved up to his large scrotum—which she could barely fit in her mouth. She exhaled hot breath while skating her tongue up and down his shaft until he was ready. Then, she stretched her lips around his thickness.

By the time Morgan put the condom on, he was so aroused that he lifted her up and jammed her down on him.

Gasping and then moaning, Morgan's juices helped her take him all the way until she was groin to groin. He sat up, partially to kiss her softly as if in thanks for giving herself to him.

Damn, did he make all his females feel like they were doing him a favor having sex with him or was he as connected with Morgan as she was to him? Every time she lifted up and returned, she found her body building up an ecstatic fever until she was burning with the desire to want everything from him.

He was mindless as well, straining to hold himself back until Morgan squeezed every muscle inside her, rocking and grinding down, bone against bone until…

His curses to the heavens was music to her ears, and she let her body receive him, rejoicing in the pleasure that drowned their souls.

She collapsed on him knowing her body weight was nothing to his strength. They were both panting in wonderment and weakened states.

Not sure who fell asleep first, but Morgan knew the rapid beating of his heart in her ear was something she would've loved to listen to forever.

***

Somehow in their slumber, Morgan had rolled to the side of him, and his condom was off his body and discarded. He was in a deep sleep and didn't wake when she slithered out of bed.

She gathered her items and went to the door of the hotel. When she was finished dressing, she could still hear him sleeping and spotted his wallet/money clip by the door.

There was a large chunk of ones, and she was tempted to open the wallet part and see his whole name.

Shaking her head, she loved the mystery of not knowing.

It wasn't as if she would ever see him again. She was through with Chicago and had no intentions of coming here again in her life.

Tomorrow morning, she would return to Detroit with the knowledge that she had the best one night stand in her life.

Slipping out of the hotel room, she asked the desk manager to call her a cab.

After she had given the driver her hotel address, she sat back with a wicked smile on her face.

As much as curiosity had been killing her to open the wallet and see his whole name, she was going to be satisfied she had kept Luke…only for one night.

…The end…

Support this author, by downloading or purchasing more books from her, reviewing this book from place of purchase and then sharing this author on your social network to encourage your reading friends to purchase her work. Thank you in advance for your support.

About this author: Sylvia Hubbard has independently published over 28 books in the genre of suspense-romance, is the founder of Motown Writers Network and The AA Electronic Literary Network, CEO of HubBooks Literary Services, runs over five blogs on a variety of subjects, host The Michigan Literary Radio Show and is a happily divorced mother of three children in Detroit, Michigan.

Considered an addicted blogger by HoneyTechblog.com, nominated and recognized for her literary work in the Metro Detroit area, referred to as "A Literary Diva" by Detroit City Council and donned "Cliffhanger Queen" by her readers, she finds solace in speaking and educating on a variety of topics.

Connect   Online   to   Sylvia Hubbard:

- **Twitter: http://twitter.com/SylviaHubbard1**
- **Website: http://SylviaHubbard.com**
- **My blog: http://SylviaHubbard.com/blogs**
- **Facebook: http://facebook.com/MichigansLiteraryWorld**

Want another book to read now? http://SylviaHubbard.com/fictionbooks

Made in the USA
Monee, IL
10 March 2020

22980159R00099